DON'T TELL
LAURA

DON'T TELL LAURA

Susan Trott

PERENNIAL LIBRARY

Harper & Row, Publishers, New York
Cambridge, Philadelphia, San Francisco, Washington
London, Mexico City, São Paulo, Singapore, Sydney

First PERENNIAL LIBRARY edition published 1987.

Library of Congress Cataloging-in-Publication Data

Trott, Susan.
    Don't tell Laura.

    I. Title.
PS3570.R594D6   1987   813'.54   86-46235
ISBN 0-06-097105-3 (pbk.)

87 88 89 90 91 92 MPC 10 9 8 7 6 5 4 3 2 1

ONE

1

Pan American's flight 125, San Francisco to London Heathrow, was forty thousand feet up in the sky, the jet making just enough noise to forbid him hearing the welkin ringing, if indeed it was. Presumably, it only rang through the sky in times of joy. No, wait a minute, the welkin was the sky, the firmament, the utmost vault of heaven itself.

Vault? It makes heaven sound like a big, Gothic building, he thought. Though a vault sounds more like something under ground. Aha! A tomb. A burial chamber. So that's why we go to heaven when we die. Anyhow, there is no joy in the world just now or, at any rate, not in my own heart – another burial chamber if ever there was one.

He was restless and uncomfortable. He hated to fly. He never could sleep on planes. Why did he fly so much? Why couldn't people come to him as the mountain was said to do to Mahomet? He had never once met an interesting person on a plane. Or anywhere.

He sprang to his feet. He would pace the aisles. He would get a drink but not talk to the stewardess which would only make him feel more discouraged with humanity.

He left first class and went into the kitchen or galley or whatever it was called.

'Can I help you, sir?'

He didn't really want a drink.

'No, thanks.'

He looked into second class where there seemed to be sitting, row on row, thousands of people!

In the first row, centre, third seat in, one of the worst seats in the lottery, neither aisle nor window, a woman slept. Her long light hair was tousled around her face. It was a nice face, an intelligent, gentle, sensitive face. He

7

loved that face. He stared at it, surprised and enchanted. It made him think of his father, and aunt, and a girl he'd known in school. It made him think of those few people in his life he had truly loved and since lost. It made him feel, despairingly, that his life was full of so many boors now. Why, oh why, couldn't he know someone with a face like this woman? Or her? Why couldn't he know her? He could. He could meet her right now by leaning over the two other people to wake her up and introduce himself and by so doing prove himself to be an outstanding boor himself.

Her body, poorly wrapped in the blue flight blanket, was slender and, even in its awkward, cramped position, looked graceful. She wore white slacks, a green jersey, an Indian bead belt. She was tanned, her hair sun-streaked. What colour would her eyes be?

His look woke her up.

Genevieve opened her eyes to find a young man staring at her. She opened her eyes because he was staring at her. How could that be? How did a look penetrate her unconscious so acutely? Why was he staring? She coloured, embarrassed. She shifted her position, pulling the blanket in such a way as to obscure her face. Even then she could still feel him looking at her. How do you feel a look, something so soundless and impalpable through a blanket?

Well, she was awake now, she might as well read. But she would wait until she felt his look go away. Too bad he had not been sitting next to her. Then, wakeful, they could have talked. Funny that she could think of talking easily with a stranger sitting next to her but wouldn't dream of hailing this stranger standing staring in the aisle.

She had imagined a meeting with someone on this, her first intercontinental flight. If he had sat by her, she could have told him about her life in the spontaneous way one is said to do with strangers one will never see again. Still

8

with her face covered, she reviewed her life now, pretending she was telling it to this staring young man. She would barely touch on the first thirty-three years – which was probably longer than his whole life – because they did not consist of the life she should have been living.

I wanted to be a runner, you see, but the schools I attended had no tracks for girls and the town and family I lived in simply didn't brook the idea of competition among women except in getting a man. Oh, tennis was all right, in a social way, but nothing to bust a gut over. No getting sweaty.

Anyhow, moving along, I got pregnant.

Here she faltered, not wishing to admit she had married without love, knowing what a terrible thing it was to have done. Her mind ranged sadly over the marriage, then she continued.

My baby was a daughter, a wonderful, wonderful girl.

At thirty-seven, I killed my husband and went to work to support myself and my child. No, just joking, just wishing. I didn't kill him, I divorced him.

Maybe I could still kill him, she thought with a high heart, and abandoned her imaginary conversation to devise ways of killing Ted Randall until she realized that her life story was more amusing. It was interesting to try to pick out the relevant parts, to have it truthful and unembellished without being dreary. Maybe it was truthful to say she'd killed Ted if that's what she wished she had done.

No, any kind of truth was impossible. If you couldn't be truthful to the person you loved most, which she hadn't been, couldn't be, how could she be to this imaginary person? She continued.

I divorced Ted. I'd already been working for years as a secretary until such time as my husband's architectural firm could get in the black. I kept working.

By the time I was thirty-nine (I know you're disappointed that I'm getting so old. I'm disappointed, too) my daughter was in college on scholarship and I had put

9

by enough to live simply, stop working and begin to race. A little late in the day, you say? No, for the masters' class was just getting going in a new world that had gone mad for running (masters being over forty). I had kept running over all the years but now I began to train in earnest and compete. I even got a coach.

How did I do? I'm so glad you asked. This year, at forty-two, I hold the American record for the masters' mile and I'm within seconds of the ten thousand metres record. It isn't too late. One really doesn't grow old this young. The body is amazing. Of course I would have been faster in my youth but my times are still improving.

Am I boring you? I thought so. It is hideously boring for a non-runner. But if I could describe the thrill of my first competitive mile at the Martin Luther King Games at Stanford stadium with tens of thousands of people looking on and me there mixing it up with some of the world's greatest athletes knowing that I, in my own, old, way, was one of them. To line up and hear the gun go off, to run my heart out and win!

They gave me a plate with a bas-relief of Dr King and this quote from him: 'I have a dream.' I was so moved, you see, because I too had a dream and it was coming true. It was a personal, self-indulgent dream compared with his but in a way I, too, was breaking open barriers, for women, older women, showing the way, the possibilities.

Now I'm going to see my daughter, Laura. She's been taking her junior year abroad at London University. I shall have a week seeing London and then we'll put packs on our backs and go off into the countryside, a precious time together.

(My life in a nutshell. Although I didn't say anything about my beloved houseboat. Or Jim, who has played rather an important role. Yes, Jim . . . but, never mind.)

I'm sorry I've blabbed on like this. I hope you will tell me all about you now. I do want to hear about you, starer that you are, potent starer, penetrator of blankets . . .

Genevieve's imaginary conversation – monologue,

rather – lulled her off to sleep so that she didn't have to imagine hearing all about him.

2

'We're just over Scotland now,' the pilot said. 'We'll be landing at Heathrow in an hour. The weather in London is cloudy, temperature sixty-two.'

Carl saw the woman standing in the aisle, looking out of the window, trying to contain her excitement. This thrill of arrival she is experiencing will make her more open, he decided. It will destroy her natural reserve as I make my big move. She will want to talk to someone and it might as well be me. The thing was not to alarm her, to let her speak first.

'See how green it is!' Genevieve exclaimed to the world at large, glancing around to see who the world was. There were others in the aisle, craning for a view. She blushed as her eyes met his. 'California is just turning gold now. Oh, but of course you know that, don't you, since you've come from California too. We all have.' She laughed at herself.

'It's all so orderly looking,' she went on quickly, as the landscape cantilevered below.

'Like a patchwork quilt,' he said mundanely, cringing at his cliché but also pleased with himself since it might make her think of him in terms of bed. 'Is this your first visit to the mother country?'

'Yes. And you? You are English?'

'Yes, but I live in San Francisco now. I've just moved there.'

'And back here so soon?'

'Briefly.' He smiled.

It was a nice smile, she thought. No, not nice exactly. It was ironic, self-deprecating, expressing amusement rather than pleasure or happiness. His face was bony,

11

long-jawed, one of those attractively ugly sort of faces. His dark hair flopped in curls over his brow. He was high-shouldered, hunched, as if from years of playing the saxophone. She would like to put her hands on his shoulders and say relax, let them fall. That would be a very Californian thing to do. He wore faded Levis, a dark blue shirt and a tan linen jacket.

He was pleased by her regard. They were silent. She looked again to the window while he continued looking at her.

Her eyes were dark brown, very dark, a surprise. Her hair was a medley of colours, even grey.

But this wasn't moving things forward. Now he could sense her growing shy again. He, too, felt tongue-tied, lip-zipped. His tongue, the most facile in the world, his mouth with its celebrated embouchure . . .

Helplessly he watched her move down the aisle to the lavatories, whither he could hardly follow her. She returned up the opposite aisle and slipped into her seat without a glance his way.

Agitatedly, he awaited the landing. He mustn't lose her.

The first class passengers disembarked first.

At the baggage claim, he pondered the possibility of offering her a ride into London. He was positive she would say no.

Suddenly she came up to him. 'Excuse me. Can you direct me to the tube from here? I'm supposed to take the Piccadilly Line.'

'Good. That's what I'm supposed to do too. You can follow me. Just a minute.'

He went over to the door where his friend was just entering.

'Great timing, Carl. The car's just outside. How was the trip?'

Ricardo Luz, despite his Mexican moniker and background, looked exactly like the stereotype Californian surfer: blond, vapid-faced, tanned of flesh and white of

12

teeth. He was short, centred, and muscular. He wore an Hawaiian shirt. He'd come on to London ahead of Carl by way of Paris. Here in London, Carl realized, Rick would stand out, look interesting and beautiful. He, himself, did not stand out anywhere.

'I'm going to take the tube, Rick. I'll get off at Kensington and taxi from there. Sorry I have to do this ridiculous thing but I do. I'm possessed. I'll explain about it later.'

'No sweat. Don't look so tormented. I love driving to and from Heathrow for no reason.' He grinned and looked over towards Genevieve. 'Good luck.'

Carl looked at Rick frostily. How dare he assume she was just a pick-up? How dare he think she was just any woman when there was no one else like her in the world?

Rick raised his hands to ward off his look. 'Hey, baby, sorry, OK? I respect your eccentric behaviour. I can tell she's unique, that this is serious. We're talking Romeo and Juliet here, right?'

'Midsummer Night's Dream,' said Carl, hastening back to the baggage area.

He grabbed his suitcases off the moving belt and put them in a trolley. They waited quietly for hers. Even though she had only one small duffel, she put it on another trolley as it seemed presumptuous to share, to have him push her bag.

Carl strode authoritatively, old London hand, down the many corridors to the underground station. He kept wanting to look back to see that she followed him but felt, Orpheus-like, that he would lose her if he did. One glance over his shoulder and she would disappear for ever into the subterranean depths of Heathrow, enslaved by its Plutonian king.

He smiled at the allusion and, at the same instant, felt worried by its aptness. He *was* Orpheus, after all. They *were* underground. He *was* leading her out.

All the more reason, then, for him not to look back, to show restraint. Restraint must be the keynote here. He

13

had realized it all along. That was why the myth had presented itself so ominously to him – as a warning to restrain himself, not to press her, alarm her, overcome her. If he did, he would lose her.

But, meanwhile, what if she weren't following him? What if, in his enthusiasm at appearing an old London hand, he'd gone too fast? Had he lost her? What if she were floundering about, feeling forsaken? Unbearable thought.

He stopped short and wheeled his trolley round, hard to do on a downslope. Her trolley crashed into his. 'Oh, I'm terribly sorry,' she gasped.

His trolley, rebounding from hers, almost knocked him down, but he recovered and grabbed his neck, crying, 'Whiplash!'

She laughed. What a wonderful laugh she had. He wanted to make her laugh again but he felt stupefied with admiration for her whoop of laughter. He himself rarely, if ever, laughed out loud.

'No good crying whiplash,' she said. 'I'm not insured.'

'How wonderful!' Everything she did, or didn't do, was wonderful to him. 'I insured my trolley to the hilt before I took one step: accident, theft, collision, fire, old age, rust . . .'

'Proceed,' she said, waving him on. 'I'll follow less closely this time. I was afraid to lose you.'

She was afraid to lose me, he exulted, practically skipping the rest of the way. We were afraid to lose each other, he thought unrestrainedly.

They bought their tube tickets. He showed her how to put the ticket in the turnstile slot and grab it again as it popped out. A train was in the the station and they got on it, he sitting across from her, not beside. The carriage was almost empty. She was surprised he sat away from her, then realized it was so he could keep looking at her. She'd never seen such a one for looking. In any case, it was too noisy to talk, except at stops. Then they had some small exchanges.

'Where do you want to get off?

14

'Russell Square.'

'That's just after Covent Garden. I shall be getting off before then, at Kensington High Street. I still have a house here (*a man of substance*). A friend is in it now (*a man with friends*). He has my car, too (*more substance*). It is on such a pretty street (*aesthetic sense*), the house, that is, and sometimes the car.' He wanted to show her the house, the street, London, his car, and through its windows all of England.

Sensing this, Genevieve grew reserved again. She was excited to be seeing Laura, having their time together, and she did not want anything or anyone to interfere. This man was very drawn to her. Men, for the most part, were. Although they were usually not so transparent about it and usually not so young.

Despite her terrible marriage, she liked men in a non-predatory way and was easy with them. They sensed that she enjoyed them without wanting anything from them, and were enchanted. So she grew reserved now, trying to disenchant.

But when the train emerged above ground and she looked down at the houses and saw the gardens, she could not help but grow warm again and exclaim, child-like, 'See all the gardens, everyone has gardens! Roses! And vegetables, too. Oh, it's so wonderful to be here. To think I never came before.' She confided, 'I love the literature of your country. I'm going to make a special pilgrimage to Jane Austen's house at Chawton.'

'My house in Kensington,' he said, 'has a garden. It . . .' The underground drowned him out. They had descended again, once again entered the vault.

At the next stop, she said tentatively, 'I've heard that Hampstead Heath is a nice place to run . . .'

'Yes, it is. It's wonderful. I've run there. Might we run together one day?'

'Well . . .' She very much doubted that he was a runner. She could tell a runner right away. Of course, he might just have begun to run. She allowed him this possibility,

15

dubiously.

'Let me give you my phone number,' he said, moving over to sit beside her. 'When you have a free hour, you could call me and we could meet.'

There, he thought. That wasn't very threatening. A harmless meeting on the heath. I can feign a sudden injury. He wrote down Carl 405 3232. Presently he would regret not having given her his last name. It was a protective tic of his, not giving his name.

She put the number in her purse, knowing she wouldn't call.

She won't call, he thought despairingly.

'How long will you be in London?' he asked. He liked sitting next to her. She had a good smell, ignited by her natural pheromones.

'A week. Then my daughter and I will go rambling down to Cornwall. She's been at London University this year.'

There is something very seductive about this young man, she thought.

'My daughter is twenty,' she said meaningfully.

Carl saw she was glad to let him know she was so old. How could she possibly think it would matter? 'I'm related to Jane Austen,' he said desperately, seeing he was near his stop, hoping still to get her interest.

What a liar this man is, Genevieve thought.

'From her brother's line,' he persisted, 'the one who took the name of Knight to continue Knight's line, though why Knight thought changing a boy's name would do that bewilders me still.'

Now she looked intrigued. At last! (Thank you, God, I'll give you a big present for this.) It was a lie, but even if she knew it was she'd still be impressed and pleased that he knew about Miss Austen's brother. It was so easy to know things. He knew almost everything there was to know – except how to get her to call him. (Also he was a little shaky on medicine and economics.)

'Where will you be staying in London?'

16

'Bloomsbury. I'll share my daughter's bedsit.'

'What is your name?'

'Genevieve.' As he had only given his first name, that's all she would do. Also, it was the California way.

'That's amazing to me,' he said. 'You see . . .' No, he would not try to tell her why her name amazed him and have to shout it above the noise of their passage. It would be revealed to her in time. Oh, God! The train was slowing now for Kensington High Street. 'Please call,' he said, standing up. He put his hand to his ear, as if to show her how to hold the receiver of a telephone. 'Will you? Please?'

She had to laugh at him holding the imaginary phone. 'I will,' she said unexpectedly.

Seeing his face light up at her promise, her heart warmed towards him. Maybe I will call him, she thought. I'll see how the week goes.

He got off. Outside, looking in at her as the train began to move, he began waving vigorously, more like a greeting than a farewell. Involuntarily, she stood up and waved back, actually got to her feet to wave farewell to him. How queer, she thought.

The train pulled away. It almost looked as if he was blowing her a kiss.

We're both behaving quite idiotically, she thought, sitting down feeling abashed, feeling the blood colour her face, feeling pleased.

Then she forgot him as she spun through the tube to Russell Square and her waiting daughter.

3

I don't know you my darling
We only just met
I've loved you for ever
I'll never forget

17

How you looked when we parted
Our paths only crossed
Briefly my darling
Two strangers who paused
An encounter by chance – two ships in the
  (K)night
Crossing and lapped by their waves and the
  bright
Rays of the moon on cerulean seas
I love you, I want you, I'm down on my knees
I don't know you my darling
We only just met
I've loved you for ever
I'll never forget
How you looked when we parted
A moment to save
You leapt to your feet
I was lapped by your wave.

Carl Knight, at his Steinway, composed this song. Strangely, it was a march, shades of Elgar, but then, magically, it would fade to a lullaby, a nocturne (as the ships passed in the night). A wild rock beat lurked in the shadows, ready to pounce. It sprang out, scuffled with the march, terrorized the nocturne, and scored.

'I like it,' said Ricardo Luz. He picked up his guitar and went through the chorus. 'I don't know you, my darling, we only just met . . .' When he'd finished fooling around with it, he said, 'Let's include it.'

Rick, only five feet five inches tall, always looked to Carl as if he were standing in a hole. But his sound was big and beautiful, even without the Mesa Boogie amp. After two years together, Carl was still surprised by how well Rick played. How did the surfing son of a Mexican migrant worker come to be such a musician? Just from playing the instrument. And listening with all his heart to the masters. And sitting in with them when he could. Rick was a wandering minstrel while Carl was out of Cambridge and Juilliard, trained within an inch of his life, a flautist. There were three other members of his band: piano, bass and drum.

'No, baby,' Carl replied, 'I'm just having fun. There isn't time to arrange it. It's just an idea. It needs work. This is a nice bit, though.' He picked up his flute, played the haunting, nocturnal passage, put it down, smiled.

'So,' said Rick, 'when are you going to see her again? Is she coming on Wednesday?'

'No. No, I don't know. She's going to call here, I hope. I pressed my number urgently upon her. That's the most I could do. Look, tell Charles, and every single person who comes here, that any phone messages from Genevieve are to be written down in capital letters and left here.' He pointed to the music stand.

'Genevieve?'

'Yes, isn't it incredible?'

'It's your first love song, you realize. I don't know how your fans will handle it, finding out you have a heart buried behind that plug-ugly exterior.'

Carl went to the mirror over the fireplace. 'Am I ugly? I never thought about it. Is it too late for surgery? Do they have whole jaw lifts as well as face lifts? What'll I do about my third eye? Just keep it closed, I guess. If only I could smile without looking like my face will fall off from trying something different.' Carl scrutinized each feature, then tried to catch the overall look. 'It isn't a hateful face, exactly. There's just a hint, the merest shadow, of winsomeness, I'd say, or is that loathsomeness? Shadows are so hard to specify. Oh, well, win some, loath some, I always say.'

Carl's look in the mirror grew more and more gloomy until Rick said irritably, 'Who cares what you look like? You're a genius.'

'I know. But now I want to be beautiful too.'

19

4

'Tell me all about him.'

Laura had just told her mother she was in love.

'You may not find him attractive at first. It took me a little while.'

They were having tea outdoors in the park in Russell Square. Beyond the greenery were ancient buildings. The Russell Hotel, a venerable pile, presided over the square. London! Gen thought happily. The long, dreary, ten-hour flight seemed now to have transported her here in minutes. And dearest Laura! She looked lovingly at her daughter. She looked pale and thinner – as students always do to their mothers, she supposed – but she looked happy.

'He's sweet and funny and smart. He likes to dance. We laugh a lot together.'

'That's good.'

'He's at the London School of Economics but he lives at the International Hall, which is where I met him.'

Some colour came to her face as she talked about him.

She was fair, like her mother, but her hair was more a true, deep blonde. She wore it twisted up on her head, precariously pinned. She was shorter then Gen and sat in composed posture. She had the gift of stillness which Gen tried to emulate. The only time Gen felt still was when she was running fast.

'He writes poetry. He went to Harvard. He'll probably be a lawyer . . .' The information bubbled out. Gen saw that her daughter was in love. She never had been before. It made Gen feel moved, somehow weepy, as if she were already at the wedding, seeing them joined.

'Then it's really serious?'

'Yes, it is. We want to spend our lives together. Is it a

cop-out, I wonder? There was so much I wanted to try to do in my life . . . it seems too easy . . . being happy, but . . . I love him.'

'You will still attempt things. I know you will. You have such a good brain and so much talent. But now you will have a companion to adventure along with. It will be easier because you will have his love and support, but it will be harder, too, because you must always consider him as well as yourself. No, it isn't a cop-out, sweetheart; it's always courageous to love someone.'

'I can't wait for you to meet him. I left a note for him to come and meet us here. He's in the midst of exams now, so he'll be tired. Did I tell you he's from Uganda?'

'No. My goodness!' Where is Uganda? Gen wondered, putting a map of Africa in her mind. All she could think of was Amin and atrocities. Now she could feel Laura's anxiety about the imminent meeting. 'I know I'll like him,' she assured her. 'If he loves you and you him, how could I not?'

How pretty she looks, all aglow. She'd always been such a serious child. Now she had bloomed.

Laura smiled at her mother. 'Tell me about you and Jim. Are you going to get married?'

Jim Lasky was an old family friend whom Gen had been seeing seriously the last half year.

'It looks like we're thinking about it. Or I am thinking, since he's decided he wants to for sure. I'm to be using this time away to reach a decision.' She smiled a little ruefully.

'He's perfect for you. He's smart, nice, supports you in your running. You have good times together.'

'All of that,' Gen smiled. 'It's true.'

'Then what's the prob?'

Gen waved the 'prob' away. 'I don't know. Maybe just the institution of marriage. I certainly do admire him and care for him. He's a good man. Did I tell you he's been asked to form his own gene-splicing company, like Genentech?'

'Ah, that was the company you made all your bucks

21

from.'

'Yes. Jim advised me to buy the stock when it came on the board at thirty-six. It went up to eighty-nine and I was one of the few who sold when it did. Now it's way back down.'

(Maybe that's why he said 'that's amazing' when he heard my name, Gen suddenly thought about the man on the plane and tube. Perhaps he is one of the Genentech boys.)

'What are you thinking, Mom?'

She and Laura were always tuned in to each other and ten months apart hadn't changed their uncanny rapport.

'A man I met on the plane. He looked rather like a mad scientist.'

'Why doesn't Jim, I wonder? He could be a banker by the looks of him.'

Gen laughed. 'I don't know. The typical mad scientist was always a physicist, not a molecular biologist. Probably they looked wild and demented because they were exploding atoms, toying with the very planet. The biologists, the recombinant DNA boys, aren't walking such a fine edge.'

'Only messing with life itself. I wonder about all this private company bit.'

'Me too. It seems it would forbid the kind of cross-fertilization of ideas that American scientists have always gloried in. Also, it seems to me that the pure research can't help but get defiled by greed. I don't like it much – now that I've made my money from it, that is.'

'How much did you make?'

'Ten million dollars.'

Laura looked stunned. Gen laughed. 'Just kidding. Fifty thousand. It will give me a comfortable cushion for a few years so I won't have to work and can keep running and whoring around – unless I get married, that is. If I get married, my cushion would be so comfortable I'd sink out of sight. I kind of like living on the edge as I do now. Not working and living on the edge, I mean. I truly hope I'll

22

never have to work again.'

'If you got married you never would have to.'

'But that's no reason to marry.'

'You love him. That's reason enough.'

'Do I? If I did, would I have to consider his proposal?'

'Mom, you were just joking weren't you? You don't really whore around?'

'Well . . .' Gen said consideringly. Wasn't there some role reversal going on here? She smiled at Laura's expression. 'No, honey, I don't. But since you've been away in college and I've been living alone, I have had some lovers, as I never did when you were under my wing. I subdued my sexuality, such as it is, for years, even forgot it existed. But I have not been in the least promiscuous, I promise you, and each man I have embraced with real affection. There were only four – and Jim makes five.' Actually there were five, she mentally amended, doing a recount, and Jim made six. But she didn't count Jim as a lover, although he'd been her first and now, if she were to marry him, would be her last. She guessed one didn't count husbands as lovers, husbands and/or the father of one's child. For Jim was Laura's real father. This was Gen's secret. Laura didn't know. When Gen married Ted Randall, he'd made her promise never to tell Laura he wasn't her father and, even after their divorce, she'd kept to her promise.

Gen scanned her daughter's face to see if Jim's features had surfaced there under the emollient cover of the London fog. No, she still looked like her mother and rather like Ted, her presumed father. Mostly she looked distinctively herself.

'I wonder where Monti could be?' Laura said, her eyes sweeping the square.

23

5

'I have been looking for you everywhere.' Gen looked up to see a slender, tall, black man, smiling, gesturing with long hands to describe the everywhere he had been looking. He was very black indeed. She had never seen a man with skin so dark, with hands so very long. She felt a slight shock, the shock of surprise and wonder, not just at his colour but at his foreignness, his exoticism, like coming upon an entirely new flower or bird after forty-two years in the field.

'Monti, this is Mom.'

They shook hands. His hand folded around hers three times. He greeted her warmly. 'How do you do? I am so happy you have come to London.'

'I am very happy to be here, Monti.'

They went on in this way, both ceremonious and loving. Then he turned to Laura to recount in detail his search for her 'everywhere' since the note she had left for him was outstandingly insufficient and vague. It would seem he had a grievance except that it was obvious he was unable to be grieved with Laura, so much did he love her, so enchanted with her was he. He could only smile upon her and translate his forlorn search for her into a merry and diverting escapade.

Laura listened, laughing. He sat down and he and Laura teased each other. A time or two Gen saw her daughter reach up her hand to gently touch his face. A caress, yes, but also an unconscious need to assure herself that he was not a chimera and neither was their love. By touching his face she came close to the heart of the matter, put her finger on the true existence of their love in a way that touching his hands could not accomplish.

His hands. Gen could not find words in her mind to

24

describe what made his hands seem so unusual. His hands, his gestures, and the patterns and inflections of his speech, all astonished her. Later, alone, she would try to recreate all these and find them to be inimitable.

And later Laura would ask her mother, 'Did you notice his hands? And his walk?'

Unlike an American black, there was no rhythm, swing, swagger or sway to his walk. No jauntiness, macho or cool, no personal statement at all. He seemed simply to float. He moved, if such a thing were possible, stilly, in the way that Laura sat, like water, clouds, or things borne on draughts of air: pollen, seeds, hawks and blossoms.

In only a few days, however, Monti was familiar to Gen, was family, was no longer exotic, so quickly does one grow accustomed to someone the heart embraces.

Conversely, Laura and Monti's love for each other did not appear more ordinary with the passage of time, but instead seemed to Gen to be ever more precious and rare, something to be observed through a glass case, to be protected by the most sophisticated burglar alarms; something to be honoured.

That Gen had not lost a daughter but had gained a son was rubbish. She had utterly lost her daughter. For years it had been the two of them, Gen and Laura. Now it was the two of them, Laura and Monti. And the one of her, she thought self-pityingly. She felt desolate, excluded. She understood that this was the natural and right way of things but that didn't make her like it.

Probably she would marry Jim. She was free, now, to think of what was best to do for herself without considering Laura first, as she always had done. And this marriage would please Laura. She liked Jim a lot, had always responded to his sincere interest in her – sincere because *he* knew he was her father. She wanted her mother to marry him, kept talking him up, saying how great he was, how perfect for her. Or had the happiness of commingling with another set Laura to proselytizing? Or, seeing herself settled, was she afraid of a lonely old age for her mother?

Gen knew there was a world of difference between loneliness and aloneness. There was a fineness to aloneness – at oneness. While loneliness fluttered and whimpered (and was self-pitying like her feelings now), aloneness was noble and still, like Monti's walk.

Gen fantasized growing old and alone. In her fantasy, her profile grew hawk-like, her body a sheath of sinew and bone.

But no. That would not do. She did not want to scare her many-hued grandchildren. She wanted, when the time came, to take them all upon a voluminous lap and hug them to her bosom beneath a beaming countenance. She could not be both hawk-like and beaming, both sinewy and bosomy. She would have to choose.

She wished she had more children. She would have loved to have had lots and lots of children, a happy marriage, but she hadn't and it was her fault – for marrying Ted, for not divorcing him sooner. But, even if she had left him when she was still young, she might have done just what she was doing now: gone off to live alone, and run races.

Jim had reappeared in her life four years ago. It had been both unsettling and pleasing. He quickly established himself as a family friend. He was still married and could do no more until now, a widower, he could marry her at last.

As Gen had pretended to tell Carl Knight on the plane, she was now living the life she should have been living all along. Jim was the man she should have married. Then. But should she marry him now? Why did she suddenly, now, here in London, have the feeling he was muscling in?

She was tempted to call Jim for some sort of surcease from thought. Hearing his voice would reassure her that what he and Laura both wanted for her was what she wanted for herself.

Briefly she thought of her ex-husband, Ted, a rare occurrence. He knew he was not Laura's father but he didn't know who was. If she married Jim, what then?

Should Laura at last be told? Gen sighed, almost groaned. She felt as if she were being physically grappled by her past.

She did not call Jim. Instead she called Carl, Carl-the-starer.

Having just come from the Courtauld Institute, a small museum of some twenty or so perfect paintings by the Impressionists – Gauguin, Monet, Seurat, Cezanne – and feeling all exalted from their company, and wanting to share her good spirits with someone, she called Carl, because Monti was at his last exam and Laura was completing a final paper.

She sauntered along Woburn Walk (where Keats had lived!) and impulsively entered the red telephone kiosk which stood out on the pavement like a sentry box.

She closed the door and studied the directions. *Have money ready. 5p or 10p.* She got out five-pence and ten-pence pieces and readied them. *Lift receiver.* She did so. *Listen for continued purring.* Got it. *Dial number. When you hear rapid pips, press in coin.* (Pips?) She dialled and was alarmed by the sound of rapid pips like a minuscule emergency police-car siren. Frantically she pressed in a coin.

'Hello?'

'Hello. May I speak to Carl, please?'

'There's no one here by that name.'

'Is this—' She repeated the number he had written down for her.

'Yes, it is, but there's no Carl living here.'

Gen hung up, feeling foolish and embarrassed. Also disappointed. Puzzled, too.

Why would he give her the wrong number? It didn't make sense. Maybe he was such as compulsive liar that he was unable to give her the right number, much as he wanted to. Even wanting desperately to give her the right number and see her again thereby, his twisted mind forbade it.

Suddenly she had a happy thought. Might not the woman who answered the phone be a cleaning lady hired

27

by the friend who took over his house – his pretty house in Kensington with the garden and the car? Lies again. Probably he lives in a bedsit like Laura or a five-by-ten room in a students' hall like Monti, with a narrow cot and a kettle to plug in for endless cups of tea.

Well, anyhow, why not call again later in the day, when the cleaning lady has gone? Cleaning lady, ha! Another of his lies.

No, it was I who invented the cleaning lady.

Later that day, covered with imaginary gore from an afternoon at the Tower of London, she found herself once again on Woburn Walk and was drawn into the same insistent phone box.

This phone box has great power, she thought.

This time she dialled with authority, was not alarmed by the pips, did not shriek 'hello' before her time, and just waited, after pressing in the money, for the woman to say her hello.

Which she did. For it was the woman, the same woman.

'Is Carl there?' Gen asked, using a different voice so as not to seem to be, at her end, the same woman, the one who had not believed her the first time.

'No, there's no one here by that name. You have the wrong number.'

Gen remembered Jane Austen's brother. 'A Mr Knight perhaps? How about a Mr Knight?' She was back to her true voice, sounding dismayed.

'I'm sorry.'

She really did sound sorry. As if she pitied her.

Gen floundered from the kiosk in the same state of mortal shame she'd experienced that morning, thinking, what an ass I am, what a complete ass.

It was a rather heavier condemnation than the situation warranted.

It is embarrassing to call a wrong number, but not that embarrassing. She must have felt that by calling this young man for a second time she was behaving childishly. It was childish and undistinguished for her to have . . .

28

hoped.

Hoped for what?

She was not sure. But it must have been for something pretty powerful – maybe the same powerful thing that had made her leap to her feet to wave goodbye to him – to feel so let down, so terribly, terribly let down, now.

6

Carl Knight entered his house and could not bear to go to the music stand to see that Genevieve had not called. He'd felt so sure she would call. Four days had gone by, more that half her stay in London, and no word.

'Carl,' called Rick, seeing him at the door, 'telephone.'

Carl slouched to the phone and talked to somebody, it didn't matter whom. What mattered was that, for the first time, he looked at the instrument and saw that the number on it was different from what it had been. It was not his number.

He concluded the conversation, suffering a combination heart attack and *grand mal* seizure, then asked Rick why the fuck the number had changed?

'Oh, apparently it rang constantly and Charles got tired of saying you no longer lived here. I'm sure I told you he'd changed it. Everyone who should know the new number does. Oh!' Rick realized why Carl was reacting so extremely. 'The woman. You gave her the old number. Too bad. That stinks, man.'

'I've lost her, totally lost her. There's nothing I can do. And what if she did call me and found the number to be wrong? What would she think of me? How explain such inexplicable behaviour – my *pleading* with her to call a number where I couldn't be found.'

Impulsively he grabbed the phone and dialled his old number. Apologetically he explained the situation to the number's new owner.

'Yes, she did call.'

'Oh!' Another heart attack. A despairing wail. 'Maybe she'll call back. If she does, will you . . .'

'She already has. I doubt if she will again.'

'Oh!' He replaced the receiver, put his head in his hands. 'Twice, she called twice!'

'We'll find her, Carl.' ,

'How?'

'We'll advertise for her. In *The Times*. Or I could walk around in a sandwich board.'

'Nine million people in London. Give me a break. I'll probably have to to Chawton, a one-horse town if ever there was one.' He cheered up, remembering her pilgrimage to Jane Austen's house. Although there was no telling when she planned to go there, it gave him some hope. 'We couldn't miss each other in Chawton. I could lie across the doorstep of Jane Austen's house so she'd have to fall over me when she arrived.'

Another member of Carl's band brought in tea, poured himself a cup and left. Rick and Carl sat down. Rick poured.

'Maybe you should let it be,' Rick suggested delicately. 'Let her go. This way you can write love songs to her until you die. If you see her again, get to know her, maybe she'll disappoint you. She may be married. Or, worse, not married!'

'No, no, you don't understand. She's different. She's so alive. She's . . . she's like me. We have an affinity. That's it, the very word. We already know each other because we *are* each other. Marriage, unmarriage, age, nationality, even sex – it doesn't matter because of this affinity. We need each other, are meant for each other. It's our karma. That's why parting after even that brief encounter was so hard. Already we were beginning to become inseparable.'

'But that's not good,' Rick said. 'If you did become inseparable, what then? Imagine losing her. And you will. Either she will leave you or she will die. And if you are symbiotically attached. . .'

It amazed Carl that someone in an Hawaiian shirt would say 'symbiotically'. Someone blond!

'Then I will die when she does!'

'You're just setting yourself up to become half a person, in that case. And, worse, a dependent person.'

'Wrong, baby, I'm half a person now. With her I will become whole. If I'm going to have a love affair, I'm not going to be wishy-washy about it. I'll be extreme. Restrained but extreme. No holds barred. What a great expression. I can try all my holds on her, bar none. If I can find her, that is.' He knocked back his tea. 'Let's rehearse the song after all. Summon the boys. I'll play it tonight at the concert. Maybe someone out there will know her. Maybe her daughter will be there. She has a twenty-year-old daughter, Rick, just right for you.'

Rick smiled and said nothing. He was a private person. Carl didn't know if he liked boys or girls or sheep. Carl didn't care and he wasn't curious. Rick's musicianship was what mattered, not his friendship, although, if asked, he supposed he'd say Rick was his closest friend.

Carl went to the piano and began to play. Then one of the band came in to remind him they had a sound check at the hall soon and should get going, so Carl gave up the idea of rehearsing the song.

It was on the return trip that he saw Genevieve. Rick was driving past the Houses of Parliament when Carl saw her running by, going in the opposite direction. She was running with an African. 'It's her! Rick, that's Genevieve!'

'Jump out,' Rick said. 'Go after her. Shout.'

Carl did neither. He slouched down in his seat. 'I can't.'

'What do you mean? Are you crazy? I will, then. Take the wheel.'

'No, stop!' Carl grabbed Rick's arm. He wanted to grab his throat, but he was always so careful of his own throat and in the thrill of the moment he forgot Rick didn't play a wind instrument. 'Don't you see – she's running. And the way she's running along with that African, well , it would be just as if someone shouted at me while I was playing in concert. It just isn't done. I mean, there she is running with Sulieman Niambui or Renaldo Nehemiah, for Christ's sake. You don't stop people like that in their practice and say, "Hi, it's me, Carl, from the plane. Remember?" '

'I just don't understand you,' Rick spluttered. 'A chance in a million – in nine million! You've been sunk in gloom for days. . .'

'It's OK. I know I'll see her again now. I'll be all right, Rick, I know. I feel so happy. Just to have seen her. Wasn't she fast? And graceful? Did you see her legs?'

'Never mind her legs. Just explain to me how you're going to meet up with her again, you jackass.'

'I can't explain. I just know I will. London's a small town, really.'

Rick thought Carl had probably decided he wanted to keep the fantasy, which this glimpse of her was enough to nourish, rather than wreck it with the reality. Carl soon got bored with women. With men, too. But his men friends didn't require or expect his interest and attention as women did. Men left him alone when he wanted to be, which was most of the time. His men friends usually had his respect, because of intellect or talent, and that sustained a relationship between them with very little interaction or, on Carl's part, caring. He was a man who inspired affection but rarely returned it. No, he couldn't pin Carl down that easily. He was a much too complicated person.

Rick glanced over at him. He was still lit up, still smiling. It made Rick smile too.

7

Past the Houses of Parliament, Westminster Abbey, Buckingham Palace ('Do you think that the Queen knows all about me?/Sure to, dear, now it's time for tea.'), Trafalgar Square – a flutter of pigeons presided over by monolithic lions, Lord Nelson a stylite. What a great way to see London, running along beside Monti who floated effortlessly, an accelerated version of his mystical walk, beside or a little ahead of her, pointing out the sights. They cruised along at about a 6:30 pace, she thought, with periodic stops at crossings which were fine with her.

Monti knew London well, threading through every little alleyway. He took her through Regents Park where the rose gardens knocked her eyes out. She would have to return when she could dally amongst them, linger and sniff. A bank of blue delphiniums astonished her, so rarely did one see a mass of flowers in blue, like the sky fallen to the ground.

Then, away they ran from the rose-scented earth, back to the stone of ancient streets and buildings. Through Fleet Street, Bleak House territory where the Jarndyce and Jarndyce case dragged on interminably. Along the Thames embankment where Quilp made an art form of squalor in his digs among the docks.

To Genevieve it was almost too much exhilaration to contain, a highlight in her ordinary life that had begun to be extraordinary in the last few years. It seemed to her that this was it, this running through London with Monti was it. It was for this, not for winning races, that she had trained.

And there was the added dimension, a kind of intimacy known only to runners, of getting to know him, to know his very breath, the very courses taken by his rivulets of sweat, while moving together through London in synch.

That night, on the phone of the woman whose bedsit Laura rented, Genevieve received a call from her fiancé. She tried to tell him of her experience that day with Monti and the thoughts she'd had, which were like a revelation. She failed. It was lost in translation. So she told him about her other sightseeing and talked a lot about Laura. 'To see Laura so happy is wonderful to me. She was such a grave child. And, oh, Jim, to see her and Monti together, it's like a dance. They're so pretty. There is such love informing every look and gesture.'

'Well,' said Jim judiciously, 'I must say you are taking it very well.'

Gen fell silent. When one has run on ecstatically about a given situation for ten minutes, rhapsodized, in effect, it is inappropriate to respond that one appears to bearing up under the awfulness of it all. She wondered if their conversation had suffered a time warp engendered by the transatlantic cable and Jim was replying to some remark in a phone call of a year or two ago.

If it was not a time warp, it could only mean one thing. 'Jim, have you a prejudice against black people?'

'Well . . .'

'Will you be happy to have black grandchildren? For that's what it comes down to.'

'It's a deep subject. Now is not the time to discuss it.'

'No, now isn't, I guess,' she said, feeling a deep sadness, a loss. 'Goodbye, then.'

'Wait, Gen, not so brusque.'

'I feel there's nothing more to say just now.'

'You could say that you love me and miss me.'

'I guess I can't say that right now. We'll talk later. Goodbye.'

'Does he miss you desperately?' Laura asked when Gen returned to the little downstairs bedroom.

'I suppose,' Gen said bleakly.

'Everything OK?'

'Yes, yes, it's fine.'

'Well, I have to go to work now. My last night. Want to come and see me at my craft?' Laura had a job as a barmaid.

'Yes, I do. What's Monti up to tonight?' Gen looked around as if wondering why he wasn't there in the little room. She was still feeling disoriented from the phone call. Abruptly, in seconds, her life had altered, and for the first time she couldn't confide in Laura. She couldn't say, Jim won't accept Monti therefore I cannot accept Jim. It would make Laura feel terrible, on all levels. Even if Gen told her, as was true, that she could not in any case love a prejudiced person, and was glad to have discovered this flaw now rather than when it was too late.

She hardly heard Laura answering, 'Monti's going to a concert. There's this musician he loves who's playing at the Palladium tonight. He's sort of London's version of Stevie Wonder – only more far out.'

'Far out? You mean new wave?'

'More his own wave. What energy. A tsunami. He calls himself – hey, know what he calls himself? GEN.'

They walked together to the Hop and Malt in Charing Cross. Gen watched her daughter draw pints of bitter for rather a rough trade. In time she left the pub and walked slowly back to Burton Street, picking up some fish and chips on the way to eat back in the room.

In the bedsit, she ate, drank tea, read *Adam Bede*, couldn't concentrate.

Need she feel so daunted? she wondered, putting aside the book. Mightn't Jim change? Probably not. He was fifty years old and prejudice was a deep-rooted thing. He would never feel comfortable with Monti, never love him or his children.

Would they see much of Monti and Laura?

35

Probably not, alas, but that was beside the point.

Mightn't Jim's love for her be strong enough to overcome this other feeling?

No, his love was not that powerful or passionate. It was a comfortable, steady love and its tranquillity would be routed and thwarted by this untoward element.

Was she right to give up Jim for Laura who virtually had given her up for Monti and Monti's world? Give up a constant companion for Laura whom now she would rarely see?

Yes, for how could she value a man who had even one abhorrent trait? She could tolerate intolerance in friends and acquaintances but not in a husband. How could such a decent person as Jim harbour this one indecency?

Well, she must give him a fair hearing, think no more about it until she went home, not let it ruin her happy reunion with Laura.

Still, what a blow.

Ten o'clock found Gen out on the street again, walking through Charing Cross.

At the pub Laura was busy. During a pause in the demand for drinks, she came over. 'Hi, Mom. What brings you back?'

'Oh, I just felt restless.'

'Stick around. You can walk me home at eleven. Usually Monti comes to meet me but I imagine the concert will go on until after midnight.'

'This musician Monti likes, the one who calls himself GEN, what's his real name?'

'I can't remember. Monti will know.'

'Do you think it's Carl Knight?'

'Yeah, I think it's Carl Knight.'

8

Rick was used to Carl's pre-concert nerves, but when the drummer looked into the dressing-room and saw Carl sitting in his underclothes, bathed in sweat, his face set in lines of incalculable misery, he exclaimed, 'What's the matter with him? His dog die?'

'He's nervous,' said Rick. 'I love him this way. It's the only time he's consistently quiet so I get to talk the whole time which I do because *I'm* so nervous.'

'When I'm nervous,' said the drummer, 'I just go around bursting into other people's dressing-rooms. But look at him. This is unique. What does he think is going to happen?'

'He thinks he's going to walk on stage in front of those thousands of people and fall down.'

Carl smiled wanly because it was exactly what he was envisioning.

'And when he tries to get up off the floor,' Rick went on, 'he won't be able to.'

How does Rick know this? Carl wondered, beginning to feel amazed.

'So then he'll decide to play sitting down on the floor but when he raises his flute to begin he'll find that he's totally forgotten how to play the thing. He doesn't know which end is which, not that flutes even have ends.'

Carl was flabbergasted. He had to speak. 'How do you know this?' he croaked.

'Because I have the same fears, you asshole. We all do. Now stop sweating and get dressed. We're on in two minutes.'

Carl walked out on the stage and did not fall down. He was deafeningly greeted by the adoring multitude. He

37

bowed to them, a relic of his classical concert days, like the formal clothes the band wore. They did not wear jackets or ties but the shirts were beautiful: pristine white, finely pleated, studded with moonstones. Collars were open and sleeves, most of them, rolled up.

They went right into GEN's theme song, 'Blue Blackbird', and from there played non-stop for ninety-five minutes, Carl transformed from the hesitant, embarrassed man who had walked on to the stage as if surprised to find it wasn't a men's room to a dazzling performer of pure, molten, white-heat energy and brilliance.

He had a way of giving his all that made each person in the audience feel he was giving it just to her or him, that only he or she understood his mind and soul and musicianship, that they weren't in a stadium but together, just the two of them, in a small room and Carl was saying, 'What do you think of this one?'

He gave a hundred and ten per cent and the group did too, all four of them feeling that with Carl they played better than their best, that he plumbed new depths of artistry in each of them just as he plumbed the depths of feeling and responsiveness in his audience.

Carl, whose pre-concert wretchedness had known no bounds, who never went a day without being tortured by feelings of fear, distrust, alienation, regret and good old ineffable, black depression, was now experiencing unadulterated happiness, one with the moment, the group, the music and the listeners. He knew that he was making his audience feel happy too. And alive! Underlying his group's great sound were their own sounds of singing, dancing, touching down with him and with each other, the pulsating sound of life, the beat of music and heart.

Inwardly he thanked them for allowing him this happiness, allowing him to give the best that was in him and so feel there was some best there to give, or some better. If he could generate all this good feeling and sound, mustn't there be something to him as a person? He hoped so. (Give

38

it some consideration, God.) Right now, his heart bursting with joy, he felt like a fabulous musician who maybe wasn't such a bad person, once you got to know him . . . and forgive him.

Although Carl had been able to rehearse his song to Genevieve, he didn't play it at the concert, again confounding Rick. He was trying to keep to his keynote of restraint, trying not to embarrass or alarm her, not to blurt out his love to the multitude before he'd even told her, trying not to look back too soon and crash into her trolley.

Although that had made her laugh. That was the moment she had warmed to him.

After the concert, Carl drove past Monti walking home but didn't recognize him as Genevieves's African running partner.

Such is the way of things, however, that Carl, in a last-ditch attempt to contact her without having to go and lie across Miss Austen's doorstep in Chawton, hung around the entrance of Russell Square tube station for a whole afternoon. He did not find her (she had taken to travelling on double-decker buses) nor did she find him, but Monti did.

There was a fruit stand at the station entrance and Carl was morosely munching his fourth apple when Monti, wandering down Marchmont Street from International Hall, saw him and approached respectfully.

'Excuse me. I attended your concert two nights ago and it was a great pleasure. I have admired your music for three years.'

'Thank you,' Carl said sincerely.

'You are the most wonderful flute player in the world.'

'Yes, I think so too. Thank you.' Carl understood exactly how good he was yet was truly grateful for any honest praise. It sometimes moved him to tears. 'What about my piano playing?'

'Forgive me if I say that it is adequate.'

Carl nodded.

'Your genius is in the totality of your music, your composition, arrangements, the way you put a song across. You have broken entirely new ground – just as the Beatles did in the sixties.'

Carl was eyeing Monti narrowly, suspecting this man to be Genevieve's running partner. His heart pounded. Again, he felt a strange reluctance to seize hold of his quarry.

'Shall we have a cup of tea?' he suggested.

'I am just going to meet my girlfriend. Won't you join us?'

'I don't want to intrude.'

'Please. It would be our pleasure.'

Carl smiled. 'Enough of this diffidence. I will brazen my way into your tea party.'

'Good. I'll just buy some apricots for Laura. She loves apricots.'

'And I will buy some scones!'

Comrades, they walked along to Burton Street, Carl talking and gesticulating, Monti attentive and regal, both in rapport, at home with each other.

As soon as Carl met Laura, he knew she was Genevieve's daughter. The same light hair and surprisingly deep, dark eyes. She was more voluptuous than her mother, and more beautiful. Genevieve was not beautiful, but she had that compelling face and such wonderful hair. How he longed to sink his fingers in her hair, which hung loose about her face, unlike Laura's which lay seal-sleek against her head.

The room was small: bed, desk, chair, bureau and wardrobe. Laura and Monti sat on the bed, Carl in the chair, each with a mug of tea, an apricot and a scone.

They talked about people who talked too much. 'It's insecurity,' said Monti. 'And nervousness. They are afraid of silence and must keep it at bay.'

'It is arrogance,' said Carl. 'They think no one else is

worth listening to.'

'If they were truly insecure,' said Laura, 'you'd think they'd be embarrassed to see you grow stony-eyed with boredom.'

'Your mother says it is hostility,' said Monti. 'She says the talker wants to hold you and trap you and beat you down with words.'

'But I feel so sorry for them. I hate to be rude and walk away. Or yawn'

'But you must,' Carl exclaimed, 'You must yawn. Your mother is right. These bores must not be brooked. They are trying to victimize you and you must fight them every inch of the way. It is intolerable to be bored. Yawn and be rude. Better, yawn and slug them.'

'Yes,' Monti agreed enthusiastically. 'As soon as they embark on a long story, hit them hard across the face.'

Laura laughed. Like her mother's, it was an open, hearty laugh.

At any moment, Genevieve might be walking through the door.

'What about people who don't talk at all?' asked Laura, who wondered why Carl Knight glanced so often at the door.

'That is arrogance too,' said Carl unequivocally.

'No, I believe that is insecurity too,' said Monti.

'It must be,' said Laura, who seemed, Carl thought, to be, unlike himself, a compassionate person. 'They must be terribly shy, painfully aware.'

'Yes,' said Carl. 'Aware of their own feelings to the exclusion of everyone else's. Self-centred. You must stop feeling sorry for these people who talk too much or too little and instead feel sorry for Monti and me who talk just enough and therefore receive no pity from anyone.'

Again the family laugh. Monti did not laugh aloud but how he smiled! My smile, thought Carl, is only a wretched flicker of the lips, as if I am afraid to show my teeth. Actually I have very nice teeth, sensational teeth.

In the last five days Carl had taken to looking in the

41

mirror. He'd grown more and more pleased with his teeth, which were nothing special, since the rest of his face dismayed him utterly. 'No wonder I don't have groupies like other musicians,' he had said to Rick one day.

'It's not because of your looks, it's because you once told them all you were gay.'

'That's right. I forgot. Then why don't I have gay groupies?'

'Because of your looks.'

Now, through the window that was mostly below pavement level, Carl could see that the day was drawing in. Although conversation continued sprightly, he felt he was outstaying his welcome and should depart.

What to do? What to say?

Should he own up to Laura that this seemingly impromptu tea party was all a vile plot to find her mother, that he'd only come to tea with that in view – the scones mere camouflage to obscure his true intention, which was to find and keep her mother.

These two had taken him to their bosoms, unsuspecting . . .

He must confess.

He should have explained at the beginning. Why was he such a devious son of a bitch?

He rose to his feet.

He would say to Laura, I met your mother on the plane. I wanted so much to see her again but I gave her the wrong telephone number. I was only hanging around Russell Square in the hope of finding her. Then Monti spoke to me and I recognized him. I had caught a glimpse of your mother running with him one day. He was kind enough to ask me to tea. I should have told you this at once. I don't know what prevented me. But I've been so afraid, all along, that anything I did or said would be the wrong thing, would lose her, and so far I've been right. I *do* keep losing her. This is my last chance. I beg you to let me stay until she comes.

'What's the matter?' Laura asked. He was standing

42

there looking tormented.

Just then there was a step on the stair. The door was pushed open and there stood Genevieve.

She started to greet them, then stopped, amazed to see Carl.

'I've been looking for you everywhere,' he said.

9

When the hubbub of greeting and explanation had died down, it emerged that it was everyone's last night in London. Gen and Laura were taking the morning bus from Victoria Station to Winchester (jumping-off point for Chawton). Monti was flying to Uganda, Carl back to San Francisco.

Gen had got three tickets for the theatre and Carl was due to dine with his Aunt Fanny.

When Laura went up to the kitchen to cook omelettes for dinner, Gen, Monti and Carl stayed in the bedsit. Carl yearned for a few minutes alone with Gen, but it looked impossible. He did not feel he could impose on their hospitality much longer, could not linger in this little room where the three of them would have to eat and change for the theatre.

Then, with every last second so precious, Gen and Monti unaccountably got into a heated political discussion. Capitalism versus socialism, no less, and thence to the difference between the French Revolution and the American. Monti said the French Revolution was a battle *for* freedom, the American simply a battle *of* freedom.

'Not true!' cried Gen incredulously. 'Why, the French didn't have battles at all to speak of. They only muscled the poor, witless, boneless aristocracy to the guillotine and whacked off their heads.'

'The French were horribly subjugated,' said Monti,

'whereas the Americans simply wanted release from their taxes on tea.'

They argued on. It seemed interminable. Carl agonized to feel the minutes slipping by. He wanted to say, look, Monti, this is simply the difference between a man from an emerging African nation and a woman from an established democracy. There is no way she can see socialism from your eyes or you the joys of capitalism from hers.

Presently there was a pause and Monti excused himself to go and help Laura in the kitchen.

Carl immediately jumped from his seat to sit by Gen on the bed.

But, distracted, she stood up. 'What does he mean?' she expostulated. 'He doesn't understand the American Revolution at all! What about eight years of bitter fighting under Washington? What about Bunker Hill? And the battle of Bennington – which I actually don't know anything about, but I went to school there.' She smiled, forgetting the Revolution, seeing Carl, noticing him.

'At last!' he said happily. 'A piece of vital information. A statistic. Tell me more. Are you married now? Do you have other children? What is your last name and your address? Is there any diabetes in your family? Congenital heart disease?'

She laughed. 'Why have you been looking for me everywhere?'

'Because of the number! They'd changed the number at my house. I felt so bad about it. I waited and waited for your call before I discovered what had happened.'

Suddenly he was afraid she would say she hadn't called, that she would lie or be coy or devious in the intolerable way that he would be. He could forestall her by saying he'd called the old number to see . . .

'I tried the number,' she said. 'Twice. I couldn't imagine why it was wrong.'

He wanted to hug her.

'May I see you when you come back to California? Where do you live? Please give me your address.'

44

'But . . . see me why? I mean . . .' She shrugged and spread her arms wide open as if to say, what is the point?

He stepped into her open arms. He slipped his hands into her hair, pulled her head to his. She resisted. He didn't notice.

He kissed her passionately, taking great handfuls of her hair into his hands, releasing one of them to run it down her spine and pull her waist to his, kissing her eyes, her nose, her neck, and again her lips which, this time, opened slightly for him, just for a moment. Then she firmly withdrew her whole body from him, looking flushed and dishevelled and absolutely adorable.

'This really won't do,' she murmured unhappily. 'What are you writing?' Carl had taken out a notebook. 'Do you think I'm dictating?'

'I'm writing down my address in San Francisco. Here.' He ripped out the page. 'Send me postcards. Three. The first from Chawton. Now' – he passed her the notebook – 'please write down your full name and home address.'

She did so, 'How old are you, Carl?' she asked as she bent over the page.

'Twenty-nine.'

'Oh, lord!' She looked up, full of dismay.

'It doesn't matter. Not at all.'

'Tell society that. I'm forty-two. I'll be forty-three this fall. And next year I'll . . .'

'I know. I grow old a year at a time, too. Granted it used to matter. If we were going to California on a wagon train during the gold rush, I'd want a younger woman who could bear me twelve kids and help me build the cabin. But it's now, I'm a musician, and I already live in California. I need a woman who can run fast. In fact, I don't *need* a woman at all. I just want,' he said tenderly, 'a woman I met on a plane and fell in love with on the tube.'

Gen blushed. She was touched, was quite won over. She felt tempted but at the same time collected enough to remind him, 'You don't know me at all.'

'Yes I do,' he said with such complete assurance that

45

she believed him, that she wondered perhaps if they'd been childhood friends.

He clasped her hand, shook it almost formally, saying, 'I'm going now. I feel embarrassed that I've stayed so long. Promise you'll send the three postcards.'

'I will,' she promised. 'Thank you,' she added, wondering what she was thanking him for. For kissing her? For not minding that she couldn't build a cabin?

He still held her hand. It felt so good, so warm and strong. She didn't want to let it go. 'It's only fair to tell you,' he said, 'that it's all over with us when I turn eighty-seven. I'll be damned if I'll go around with a hundred-year-old woman.'

She laughed and they kissed goodbye passionately because the laughter released her from her previous constraint. How could you hold back from a man who made you laugh, who gave you such a gift?

Or maybe she allowed herself this good giving and taking kiss because she didn't believe they'd meet again. This was one of those chance encounters complete in itself where the fervour degree of kisses didn't count.

As Carl went up the stairs, he could hear Monti saying to Laura, in a humorous way, 'Politically, your mother and I are diametrically opposed.'

But Laura answered him with a statement from her own thoughts. 'I think Carl should have told us he was looking for Mom. If he knew who we were, it wasn't right for him to pretend he didn't.'

'We don't know that he knew.'

'He knew,' she said – sourly, Carl thought.

He came to the kitchen door. 'I want to say goodbye and thank you for tea.' He looked chagrined. 'I overheard what you just said, Laura. You're right.'

'It isn't that I want to be right, it's that I wish you hadn't done it.'

'I wish I hadn't, too,' he lied, trying to appease.

She was protecting her mother. She had, he saw, entrenched herself against him. She disapproved of him.

46

What do you want with my mom, her look seemed to say.
'I hope I'll see you both back in the States,' he said.

'I hope so, too,' said Monti warmly.

'You must meet Jim Lasky,' Laura said, cracking eggs
into an orange plastic bowl. 'Mom's boyfriend. They're
engaged to be married.'

Carl felt a moment's anguish, then fortified himself. Of
course she has a boyfriend, he thought. How could she not
have a boyfriend? But need Laura have said it? Had his
coming to tea been so odious an act? Hadn't he helped her
to understand about over-talkers and non-talkers?

He armed himself. If Laura wanted to fight, they'd
fight. The troops were mustered, swords were drawn. He
remained silent until she looked his way, waiting to wither
her with some ultimate remark. But she never looked his
way, instead whisked eggs.

Fuck off and die, he could say. But might that not cause
a rift that could never henceforth be breached? Would
Genevieve be pleased?

'I'll see you out,' Monti said, getting up, easing him
away from the kitchen door. It was too kindly to be called
the bum's rush, but still . . .

The next thing he knew he was outside in Burton Street,
the withering remark withering on his tongue, his famous
tongue. Never mind, he thought, buoying himself up. I
found Genevieve, I have her address, she kissed me, she's
going to send me postcards. So what if her daughter hates
me.

He met his Aunt Fanny at an indifferent Indian restaurant near his house in Kensington.

'I hope you are going to give up this silly idea of living in
San Francisco, Carl,' she began, once they were at their
table. 'It's so new there. I went once and felt all the time as
if I were standing on shifting sands. When I got back to
London I went straight to Westminster Abbey so that I
could feel thousands of years of stone beneath my feet and

47

be steadied.'

'It wasn't just stone you felt, it was bones. That's what I love about San Francisco. They don't bury men in churches there. And the sky is blue almost all of the time (I know that sounds preposterous) and in society you are respected for your achievements or contribution rather than who your family is.'

'How horrible. I'd have been nobody there. Good blood is such a comfort.'

Carl smiled at his aunt. She looked every inch the English lady, but the family blood was not as pure as all that. Happily the Anglo-Saxon had stood back to allow Semetic and Arabic genes into his system to flourish there and produce his musical and poetical talents. He smiled, too, because he saw his father's beloved lineaments in his aunt's face.

His father had been dead for four years. Fifteen years before that he had divorced Carl's mother, keeping Carl to raise by himself. Carl's mother had got married again – to a woman.

His aunt, although professing to be a non-achiever, was a breeder of champion Airedales, a power in the Kennel Club circuit.

'How are the pups?' he inquired now, and she told tales of the latest litters, dwelling chiefly, however, on the rare illness of her champion bitch, Stargazer of Stonehedge (her kennel). Carl felt relaxed for the first time in days. He had found his Genevieve, secured her. So he leaned back and listened tranquilly.

'What are you grinning about? I was recounting a hideous death.'

'Oh, sorry. I'm grinning because I'm in love.'

'I thought you seemed a little queer. So that's why you've moved overseas: you've met someone.'

'I guess I did move there so I could meet her whilst flying back here.'

'Tell me all about her.'

'She's a runner,' he said proudly, and because that was

48

all he knew about her.

'Oh? A runner? Do you mean competes in races, like the Olympics?'

'I don't know if she's that good. Only the best in the world run there, you know. In any case, she's too old to compete on that level. I only saw her once again, after our initial encounter, and that was briefly.'

'So you're in love with an old runner. How interesting.' Aunt Fanny rolled her eyes. 'How bizarre.'

'She's not that old. Not *decrepit*.'

She smiled. 'She couldn't run if she were.'

'She has a lovely daughter,' he said, remembering another fact to tell, 'who's in love with a Ugandan. I met them both today.'

She surprised him by saying, 'Uganda is the pearl of Africa. I should love to go there one day. I believe their game reserves are the nicest of all. How is your music, Carl?'

'The music is good but the life is hard. I have no life. It is only practise and rehearse and hit the road and play and try not to go mad.' Carl closed his eyes for a moment and was still.

Aunt Fanny looked concerned. 'Carl, do you go to church any more? You used to be so devout.'

'No, God and I have lost touch. Well, not entirely,' he amended. 'We sometimes connect in a cursory way, send bulletins and so forth. I've lost His favour now that I'm so vain, selfish and materialistic. I'm trying to win Him back but He doesn't seem to have a price. He seems to expect me to change.'

He lifted his glass, smiling. 'But never mind that. I want to tell you more about my old runner.'

'I believe you're making it all up to amuse me. You've never fallen in love before. Why should you now?'

'It was love at first sight.'

'That's how it was with your father,' she said direly. 'They met in a revolving door.'

'I never knew that. It makes my meeting seem so mun-

49

dane.' Carl wished he could meet her all over again. Still, forty thousand feet up wasn't so shabby. And the way he'd wandered back from first class and seen her. And then, forswearing his car to go with her on the tube was very romantic, really. They'd met in the sky and he'd won her underground, all in an hour. Then he'd found her again in a room that was half underground, half above, and clasped her in his arms!

Remembering their kiss, his sex began to swell but sallied down again as he remembered Laura. It certainly was too bad about her not liking him. He must win her over somehow. Maybe he could give her money, *buy* her love and approval, an approach which, unlike God, humans were open to. Or, better, beat it out of her. After all, if one should hit a boring person to stop him talking, why not hit a recalcitrant person to start her loving? Buying or beating a person is so much quicker than devoting months to proving what a decent person you are – especially if you're not a decent person, which he might well not be.

'Do you think I'm a decent person, Auntie?'

'You are civilized, reliable, kind to those *few* persons you care for, generous. I think those attributes can define decency. You are a man of high feeling, certainly. You do act up at times. For a musician, though, you are quite intelligent . . .'

'Intelligent? What do you mean, intelligent? I'm a genius!'

'Well, my dear, geniuses aren't always intelligent. They are often simply extremely good at one thing.'

'That's absolutely ridiculous. It's a myth. Geniuses are the most well-rounded people in the world. People also think geniuses are physically frail and uncoordinated whereas they are usually far better athletes than the norm. Ben Franklin was a superb distance swimmer. Einstein was an unusually strong man and a good sailor. They say Newton had carpenter's hands.'

'Einstein was physically strong, yes, but a gentle,

50

tranquil man. Like all geniuses he had an abnormally strong ego but he totally subdued it. You let yours rip.'

'Einstein was dedicated to pure thought. It was for him to determine the nature of the physical universe. In order to do that he had to get out of himself, get his ego out of the way and be all pure throbbing brain. But I am a man of passionate expression. I need my ego.'

'Then it is bound to sometimes get in the way of your being thoroughly decent – to get back to your original question. Are you worried whether your lover will think you're decent?'

'No, not her, her daughter.'

'It shouldn't matter what she thinks.'

'It shouldn't, but sadly I fear it will. Those two women are preternaturally close.

10

'I don't like him,' Laura said.

She and Gen were at the Greyfriars Pub in Chawton, having tea, and Laura had noticed that her mother was writing a postcard to Carl.

'I am so moved to be here in Jane Austen's town,' she wrote. 'I just walked down the road to the church as she must have done each Sunday. Nothing is changed. It could still be the eighteenth century. Roses everywhere. I saw a field of pigs. We don't have green fields full of pigs in America. They're kept in mud. This pub is as cosy as pubs are said to be – but never were in London. Gen.'

Gen looked up. 'Don't like who?'

'Carl Knight.'

'Why ever not?'

'I don't like his humour, his looks. I don't like it that he didn't tell Monti and me he was looking for you. It seemed sly. I don't trust him.'

'Well . . .' Gen felt hurt.

'Why are you writing a card to him?'

'He asked me to.'

'So?'

'What do you mean, so? What's the matter with you? He's just a guy I met on the plane. He's nice. I like him. I can write him a postcard if I want.'

'How would Jim like it? Do you want more tea?'

'Yes, please.'

Laura got up and went to the bar. Gen stuck out her tongue at her daughter's back. Maybe I should please her by writing a postcard to Jim, she thought. I could tell him, too, about the pigs. All those astonishing, spanking-clean pink pigs in a bright green field. What a sight. I could say there were black pigs too, and among them some baby brown ones. No, I'm just too sore at heart to write to Jim at all.

The second postcard to Carl she wrote while by herself on the bank of the river Avon in Salisbury, close to a lone angler, at dusk.

'I have discovered a new hero, William Walker. He saved Winchester Cathedral *with his own bare hands*, working underwater for five years in total blackness, in a turn-of-the-century, two-hundred-pound diving outfit, shoring up the tottering foundation.'

The postcard had a picture of William Walker on it, looking stalwart and bemused. She hoped Carl wouldn't already know about him, that this would be fresh news from the English countryside of seventy-five years ago. But, for all she knew, Carl could be from Winchester, even part of the Walker family on his mother's side – since his father's side was, ostensibly, Miss Austen's.

There was still some room on the card. 'Tomorrow Stonehenge,' she wrote, 'then onwards to Cornwall. Gen.'

Pretty dry all in all, she thought, reading it over. Between Cornwall and Gen she inserted the word love. That would make it a little more juicy.

She remembered their embrace, remembered with her

whole body as well as her mind. She moaned aloud. Then she looked round, embarrassed, to see if the angler had heard. He hadn't. He was absorbed in the stream and the line's entry into the water like a needle through cloth.

She got up, walked on, to the youth hostel where she and Laura were staying. William Walker, she thought, wasn't heroic so much as damned tenacious. Would Carl want me to admire such a man, plodding along in his weighted boots, faithful labourer, carrying concrete blocks and bricks through the watery darkness, the water itself all sicklied o'er with germs from the graveyard beneath the church? Not a man of much art or imagination. A beast of burden, really, but noble somehow, I think. He was proud to do the job. He told the King later, when the King commended him, 'I'm proud to be able to help in so grand a work.'

The third postcard she wrote a week later from Fowey, but by then the brief encounter with Carl had receded. He had no real existence for her. It was Jim she was thinking of once more. Jim and their satisfying relationship, their knowledge, understanding and appreciation of each other, the bond of their loaded history. Perhaps she'd misunderstood him on the phone.

She had just finished quite a long run and still had almost three miles to cover along the railway tracks from Fowey to Golant where their youth hostel was, a beautiful mansion high on a hill by the river. She was having a hot cup of tea on the pier as the air was chilly and she'd picked up a pretty postcard of the town.

'Dear Carl, I've just run the footpath along the cliffs from Fowey to Polperro and back. It was exhilarating. Purple foxgloves everywhere and the endless blessed sea.'

She paused and couldn't think of one more thing to say. She couldn't remember what Carl looked like or who he was and why she was writing to him at all except that she'd promised three cards and if there was ever a woman who kept her promises it was she. He was a stranger she'd met on the plane whose arms, for some reason, at their

53

next meeting, she'd fallen passionately into, whose mouth she had tenderly kissed. She'd followed up this unsuitable behaviour by thanking him and promising postcards.

She shook her head wonderingly and instead addressed the card to Jim, adding, 'I'll be seeing you in four days. Till then, love, Gen.'

She forgot to alter the 'Dear Carl'.

TWO

1

Gen lived in Sausalito, the first town north of San Francisco, on a houseboat. Here she continued her pursuit in her forties of all the things that a hasty marriage had deprived her of in her twenties and the daily grind had disallowed in her thirties.

Three years ago, when Laura left for college, Gen had moved out of the San Francisco apartment they had shared together, left her secretarial job and, with her windfall from the stock market, bought a ten-speed bicycle and a small but pleasing living space where she could run out of the door and along the marshes, up a nearby mountain, or over the bridge to the city. She had enjoyed five lovers, serially, and now, completing her lost twenties, she had travelled abroad and stayed in youth hostels.

She had achieved her running ambitions, exulted in the freedom of her own days with no work to go to or demands made on her by any man or child.

Having experienced all this, it was conceivable that she could now marry again. Except that she liked this life. She liked her small, own space, her running, her friends, independence, and aloneness.

But how would it be in her fifties, sixties? She did not want five more lovers or even one more. She had a distinct and tender memory of each one. Beyond five it seemed to her the blurring would begin.

Jim was a catch. Everyone agreed. As well, she loved him and Laura did too. He'd been a family friend for years. They had been together as a couple for six good months. He was rich and he was successful. He travelled a good deal and so encouraged her independence. He approved of her running even if he did not thoroughly

57

understand it. He was a physical person himself (tennis, skiing), was intelligent, kind. And prejudiced.

He met her at the airport and they had already broached the dread subject on the drive back. He didn't seem to take it very seriously, which amazed her, and (more amazing) he couldn't understand why she did.

She looked at him, a handsome sandy-haired man, with a keen glance and amiable expression. 'But why?' she asked, feeling painfully distressed. 'How can you be prejudiced, a man as intelligent as yourself, a man of the world?'

'Prejudice has nothing to do with intelligence. It's completely unreasonable. It is a matter of feelings, not thoughts or experience or knowledge. You know that. And, although it's true that the *idea* of Monti throws me for a loop, I'll probably find him to be the finest fellow in the world and we'll get on splendidly.'

'But it isn't just a matter of getting on – Laura could easily marry someone you wouldn't get on with – it's the idea of prejudice being in you that so deeply disturbs me.'

'Can you honestly tell me that you are completely without prejudice?'

'Yes.'

'What about Hitler?'

'That's not prejudice, that's hate. And it's not just Hitler,' she added, 'it's the whole Nazi regime. My hatred isn't based on an unreasonable prejudice but on a true clash of values.'

'You can't forgive the holocaust and you're not even a Jew,' he said, still being slightly facetious.

'But that's just it. One doesn't need to be a Jew, good God! to feel the horror.'

'I know,' he said seriously.

'Oh, how beautiful it is!'

They were crossing the Golden Gate Bridge. The tower ahead was silver, not orange, being sandblasted for the never-ending paint job. The orange cables reached up into the high fog, disappearing there like an Indian rope

58

trick.

Presently they wound down Alexander avenue, the narrow road to Sausalito. They continued through the town, parked at the bait shop and walked the pier to Gen's gangplank.

Gen felt the combination of fondness and embarrassment she usually experienced whenever she took a detached look at her home. It was so cute. The window shutters, for instance, had hearts carved out of them. There were window boxes which insisted on geraniums, petunias and lobelias, while above the door was a stained-glass window portraying bluebirds (of happiness) fluttering amid a morning glory vine. There was even an American flag, which Gen had no particular intention of letting wave any more than she thought she would plant the window boxes but she did. So Old Glory adorned the air above the boat and she, quite properly, took it in each night at sundown and pulled it up the little pole at dawn and set it at half-mast whenever a good person died. A neighbour, probably old Ben, had raised it for her return today. To complete the cuteness of her home, there was a cat, calico of course, who wandered by one day and stayed. She named him Glory, to go with morning and old. He, basking on the threshold, greeted her nonchalantly, and walked away.

Inside was a minimal kitchen, a small living-room, and a tiny bedroom with a deck off it about the size of four chess boards. From the deck was a view over Richardson Bay to Mount Tamalpais in Mill Valley, which was the next town north.

Inside, as well, on this day of her return, was a vase with a dozen yellow roses. Her favourite flower. How did he know? The card said, 'Welcome home. Please call me at this number: 922-6855. The number is current as hell. I even installed a recording machine in case I'm out when you call so the thing is foolproof. But I'm not out. I'm sitting next to the phone even as you read this. Carl Knight.'

59

It was true about the number and the machine being installed, but Carl Knight was not sitting by the phone. He was in hospital with a heroin overdose.

Rick, hunched in a chair by the bed, looked as if his own body had taken the blow. His face was grim. 'Do you know how close you came? Do you?'

Carl's response came dismally, in the frailest of voices. 'The stuff was powerful. It had only been cut ten times instead of twenty. The guy told me it was potent but I didn't believe him. That's the trouble with being a liar, you never believe anybody else.'

'I thought you were off the stuff. I thought you decided you didn't have to die young to be a legend.' Rick sounded angry because he'd been so scared. Now that Carl was going to live, he wanted to kill him.

'I didn't want to die. I just wanted to say hello to The Bird.' Carl smiled at the thought. Then he tried to reassure Rick. 'I'm not an addict. I'm only an occasional user. You know that. The stuff doesn't have me in its vice-like grip. I'm in control.'

'For an occasional user, it only takes one occasion,' Rick said thinly, then he shouted: 'You went into a goddamn coma, man! You were hardly breathing!'

'It was my last big bash before embarking on the clean life with my runner. Oh, my God! What day is it?'

'Never mind.'

'She's back, isn't she? Has she called?'

'You unplugged the phone when you went on your trip. That was two days ago.'

'I've got to get out of here.'

'I don't think you'd want her to see you looking like a cadaver. Give yourself a chance.'

'Will you go and find her? Tell her . . . anything. Make up some reason why I'm away. Tell her I'll call. Please?'

'I will.'

'Good. Thank you, baby. I sent her roses. They'll be there to greet her. I'm so glad I sent her roses. Oh, Rick, why did I do it? Why? I'm so miserable. I'm such a

60

miserable, fucked-up asshole.'

'It's because you're such a vulnerable asshole. You're afraid. Every time you have a success like you just did in London, you feel overwhelmed. You feel you don't deserve it, even though you've worked your whole life for it. Even though you're one of the few truly innovative musicians around. And, probably, you're afraid to love this woman, much as you want to.'

'Oh, baby, I'm so down.'

'It's the Nalline, too. It's a despair drug. It's the antidote for heroin and therefore also the antidote for ecstasy. Also, you're probably hungry. Here, have some intravenous feeding.

2

'So,' said Jim Lasky, reading the card, 'you found yourself an admirer in England.'

'I met him on the plane and only saw him again once, by chance.'

'It must have been quite a meeting,' he commented idly. At the same time, he flashed her a penetrating look.

In spite of herself, Gen blushed.

'Tell me about him.'

'He's an English musician who goes by the name of GEN. Have you heard of him?'

'No.'

'Neither had I. I guess he's better known in England. He's just moved to this area. That's all I know about him.'

As she talked, she unpacked, putting her dirty clothes in a laundry bag, her clean in the closet. Her place was so small that the suitcase left on the floor would make it hard to move around.

Jim got himself a beer from the refrigerator. She could tell he was unthreatened by the roses. He was confident, mature, rational. Wasn't she glad? Wasn't this the way she would want a man to be? Wouldn't it be deplorable if he made a fuss, tossed the roses overboard, sulked?

'Are you going to call him?'

Gen paused in her unpacking to to address herself to the question and answer truthfully.

She was touched by the roses. Who would not be? It was a shame. Here was Jim, her steadfast, true friend and fiancé, who had taken two hours from his busy schedule to drive heinous miles at an ungodly hour to fetch her from the airport. But all that kindness paled beside Carl's effortless, one-minute-long gesture of sending her the roses. The roses were so beautiful, so extravagant, romantic, impetuous. They looked luminous in the early morning light.

'Or are you going to marry me?'

'May I have more time, Jim? It hasn't to do with the roses at all. It has to do with Laura and Monti.'

'What does Laura think of our marrying? Did you discuss it with her?'

'She likes the idea very much. She loves you. She wants us to be together.'

'Her feelings should clinch it, I should think, loving Laura as you do and, I trust, loving me as you do.'

'But Laura doesn't know about your . . . prejudice.'

'Oh, for pete's sake,' he said irritably. 'You make it sound like a disease.'

'A disease I could handle. A disease could get well. Right now it colours' – she smiled bitterly – 'bad choice of words, my feelings towards you. I can't help it, it just does. I have to work it through in my mind. I thought I knew you as well as I knew myself. Now I have dicovered this stranger in you (this monster, she thought) and so I have to reassess everything.'

He looked deeply hurt. Her heart gave a twist and she reached out for him. She felt him want her and responded at once – physically but not mentally.

No, it isn't right, she thought. Hungry as I am. She

drew away. 'I'm sorry.' She felt small. They had been three weeks apart. He'd come to get her. He looked at her as if he'd discovered a monster in her. She hung her head, feeling terrible.

'I'll be going along, then,' he said drily.

He glanced at the roses as he left.

It has nothing to do with the roses, she wanted to shout after him. It has to do with human dignity!

Damn, he will think this is about Carl Knight. And it isn't. It isn't at all.

The glance Jim had given to the roses as he departed assumed mammoth proportions, grew more and more loaded.

She felt wronged and misunderstood.

He is saying my feelings have changed towards him because of this boy and that I am just using his prejudice as a lever to extricate myself. He demeans me.

She grasped the bouquet and lifted it from the vase. She carried them, dripping water, to her deck and threw them into the bay. They floated, lilies without pads, glimmering yellowly on the silver-misted water. An egret flew by on angel wings, immaculately white, his legs flung out straight behind him. 'Cronk!' he called.

What a grand thing to say, thought Gen.

Rick, asking directions to her boat, looked the way of the gesturing hand, saw her throw the roses in the water, and decided it was pointless to go any further.

Gen went back inside. It looked forlorn without the roses, but gradually her heart lifted. It was nice to be home. Glory reappeared and neighbours dropped by, now that Jim had left. Every one of them asked where the yellow roses had gone. They all knew they had been delivered and that Old Ben had put them in a vase for her.

Finally Ben himself arrived with seven of the roses. 'I didn't think you meant to throw these in the water, so I got them back for you, went out in my dory. Better wash off the salt. Probably Jim got you to feeling bad about them. But they're awfully pretty and I know you love yellow

63

roses.'

'Oh, thank you.' She gave him a warm kiss. 'I'm so glad you rescued them. It was a crime to throw them out.'

Ben lived on the next houseboat. Except for the usual cataract operations and arthritis problems, he was well muscled and strong-hearted for a man of eighty-odd. He'd lost his wife a year ago and her sister had been on the verge of coming to live with him when Gen had gone off to England.

'Did your girlfriend come?'

'I expect her soon. It's just an arrangement, you understand, so we can look out for each other. At my age, there's no question of sex.'

Gen and the others laughed. Ben had said this often enough to give them all the feeling that there must be a question or he wouldn't be thinking about it so much. They liked to quote it to each other whenever discussing a new relationship. At my age, Gen had said of Jim and herself, you understand that the question of sex does not arise. In fact, it's a foregone conclusion that we'll have lots and lots of sex.'

Ah, those were the good old blithe and happy days with Jim, Gen thought (although, come to think of it, their sex had been infrequent).

Her best friend, Sally Morain, bicycled over from Ross, the other side of Mount Tamalpais where she lived in her family mansion. She was thirty, and the fastest woman runner in the Bay Area. She radiated health and beauty with rosy cheeks, sparkling blue eyes, and gleaming blonde curls.

The two women hugged each other.

'Ready for a run? You can tell me all about England as we go.'

'Great. A run will set me to rights. The very thing. You can tell me all about your latest big tall lover.'

Sally liked large men but most male distance runners

64

were slight. If she dated a non-runner, big and satisfying though he may be to her senses, he didn't understand her lifestyle. If by chance she found a runner who was big enough, he was usually nowhere near as fast as she was and couldn't handle her superiority.

'I think I've solved my problem,' she said. 'I'm looking at the ultra-distance runners now, the hundred-milers. They're all built bigger for endurance. Trouble is, they're all pretty brain-damaged.'

'That's the trouble with solving problems, the solutions usually create new ones. Maybe you can solve my problem . . . '

And Gen told Sally the saga of the morning with Jim as they ran ten miles of trails through Tennessee Valley and the hills on either side of it.

'I know GEN's music. I have a record of his. In fact two records, one when he was a classical flautist and soloist with a chamber orchestra. He's fabulous. I guess he felt classical flute was confining, the repertoire being so limited, so he burst into jazz. Still, it's such a different world, it must be hard . . .'

'Sally, this is interesting, but it's not solving my problem.'

'It's hard to see being loved by two guys as a problem. Anyhow, my suggestion is do nothing. Wait and see what happens. Be an observer. Let Jim and Carl figure it out and make the moves.'

'That's one of those wonderful, totally unworkable suggestions.'

'That's the whole idea – not to work at it. It's sort of a no-suggestion. You Zen it.'

Gen stopped talking as they ran up a steep incline. Sally floated effortlessly on up the hill in front of her while Gen struggled and gasped. She realized that while in England she had got out of condition.

'I'm so out of condition,' Carl complained to Rick four days later. 'I've forgotten how to breathe. I've lost my

65

tone float. My air is coming from my throat instead of my toes. For every day of practice I lose, it takes three to recover. Five hours a day it's been for twenty years. That means I have thirty-six thousand five hundred to go for another twenty. You know, Pablo Casals came here when he was twenty-four and went hiking on Mount Tamalpais. A falling boulder smashed his fingering hand, and do you know what he thought as he looked at his bloody, mangled mitt?'

'What?'

'Thank God, I'll never have to play the 'cello again.'

Rick looked shocked. It made Carl feel old – as old as Casals felt at twenty-four.

'I always think of what Jack Teagarden said about practice,' Rick said encouragingly. ' "I try to play better tomorrow than I do today." Anyhow, I'm glad to hear you bitching about your breath. It means you're your old self again.'

'You damn guitarists,' Carl said querulously, 'you don't understand because you don't have to breathe.'

Rick laughed, then Carl laughed too. He suddenly hugged Rick. 'You're the best friend in the world. Thanks . . . for always sticking by me. For not giving up on me.'

But the happy moment passed and Carl's face resumed its woebegone lines. 'If only I could understand, Rick, then I could let her go in my mind. If I could just ask her why. There could be a reasonable explanation.'

Rick shrugged. 'It's hard to think of one. Damned hard.'

'Tell me again exactly what happened.'

'When I left the hospital, I went to her houseboat to tell her you were called away suddenly and would get in touch with her when you got back. I found myself on the wrong pier and asked someone where her houseboat was. He pointed across the water, saying, right over there. That's her on the deck. She just got back from England.

'I looked where he was pointing and saw Gen – it was

66

definitely her — throwing your roses overboard. They weren't dead. They looked fresh and nice.'

'Then what?'

'Then she leaned on the railing watching them for a bit. There didn't seem any point in my giving her the message, the bitch.'

Carl blew a long, soul-filled note on his flute. The ancient call of the shepherd to his sheep. He imagined them hurtling up the hill to him while he held the note, lambs and rams and ewes all in their dumb number, he in his jerkin.

'There. That was right. It's coming back.' He sat silently a minute. 'Just threw them overboard. I don't think I've ever felt so hurt in my life. You're right, Rick, there's nothing more to say or do.'

'I'll see you later.' Rick evaporated from the room. So little and lithe was he, he came and went with no commotion.

Carl lifted his flute. As he played, he remembered, 'If music be the food of love, play on. Give me excess of it so that surfeiting, the appetite may sicken and so die.'

He played on for another half an hour. 'That strain again! It had a dying fall. O it came o'er my ear like the sweet sound that breathes upon a bank of violets, stealing and giving odour. Enough! No more: 'tis not so sweet now as it was before.'

Might she, he wondered, again ceasing his practice, have somehow learned about my overdose and been so disgusted that she flung the roses from her presence lest, stealing and giving odour, they poisoned her environment as the heroin poisoned me? Rick kept it from the press, admitted me into hospital under an assumed name. Still, these things get out. I can't call her and ask, is it because of the heroin, Gen? Do you think I'm a vile junkie? I never said I *wasn't* a heroin user. It's not as if I lied to you—about that. It's true I'm not related to Miss Austen. I'll never do it again. The heroin, I mean. I had excess of it. Surfeiting, the appetite sickened and so died. Luckily just before I so died. Just barely before so. But it would help me so much, Gen, to keep going, if you'd love me. I'm a lot like your William Walker the diver who saved Winchester Cathedral with his bare hands. If he captured your imagination, I could too. That's what love is, capturing a person's imagination. I keep at a thing intrepidly like William Walker. I play the flute with my bare hands. I want to love you with my bare body and my bare brain. You'll love my brain, once you get to know it, and learn to ignore my personality. I wonder if you realize how you continued the underground theme of our love affair with that postcard, carried it to new depths, took it under water.

But all this is no good. Facts are facts. She threw away my roses and there's nothing more to say or do. He lifted his instrument, played an arching, dying fall.

3

A week passed. Gen followed Sally's advice and did nothing. No one else did anything either. She heard from neither Jim nor Carl. She felt a rat not to have thanked Carl for the roses, but she was in a dilemma. She did not want it to appear, even to herself, that she had dumped Jim for Carl.

One morning she was pottering about her boat, watering the flowers in the boxes, picking off dead heads and leaves, with Old Glory fluttering above her and the cat Glory winding between her legs like a slalom practice, when the telephone rang. Wiping her hands on her jeans, she went to answer and it was Jim.

'I just wondered if you'd seen your new friend Carl Knight since you got back?'

'No, I haven't.'

'Probably you were unable to reach him.'

'I didn't try.' Small satisfaction that she could say this honestly – but small was better than no.

'He was in hospital here at the medical centre.'

'Oh dear . . .'

'On a heroin overdose.'

'Oh!'

'He's home now. Close call. I don't think you ought to get mixed up with someone like that.'

'Jim, I'm not planning to get mixed up with him. He is someone I met on my travels. I wish you would understand . . .'

'I'm going to China for a few weeks,' he interrupted.

'You are?'

'Yes. It was a trip I wasn't going to do, but now I think I will. With things as they are . . .' He paused. 'Are they any different?'

'Not really. No. I guess not. I . . . I miss you. I feel sad that you're going away. But, well, Laura will be arriving in a fortnight. Maybe I should talk it all over with her. I never did in London. I didn't want her to know. Still, ultimately, it's my decision.' Gen foundered. She wasn't making any sense. And why in the world had she said the English 'fortnight' instead of two weeks? He would think she had been seeing Carl when she hadn't – she'd only been thinking about him incessantly.

'I should have thought you'd feel gratified that I can overcome my prejudice, that this feeling doesn't stand in the way of my love for you and my desire to marry you, that it never once made me falter in my decision and my promise. Whereas you . . . at the drop of a hat . . . as if seizing the chance . . . and not because of anything I've done or not done . . .'

Obviously he'd been doing a lot of thinking this week. His feelings towards her were bitter. Good plan of Sally's, this doing nothing. Gives people time to grow to hate you.

Gen wanted to say she was sorry. But for what? She was only trying to be true to herself. However, she *was* sorry he was feeling so hurt and wronged, sorry to have been the

69

cause.

'I hope you have a nice trip, Jim.'

'I will. Maybe when I return you'll be over your infatuation.'

Gen realized he'd rather think her withdrawal was because of Carl and not because of some flaw she'd discovered in him. She also knew he was being irrational but had every right to be because of his hurt.

'Junkies usually aren't prejudiced,' he added.

'That's a ridiculous thing to say.'

'I know. I guess I'm also prejudiced against junkies. But even if I were still only your friend I'd advise you to have nothing to do with that man. It will just mean a lot of trouble and heartbreak.'

'You don't believe that I haven't seen him, do you?'

'I know that you will. I know you.'

Gen hated someone to say I know you. The implication was not I know how wonderful you are but rather I know what a fool you are. But she understood that by taking this tack he was trying to put her on the defensive and thereby exact some sort of promise that she would not see Carl. Then she'd be bound not to. Whereas, now that she'd learned of his tragedy, she felt it incumbent upon her to call him.

'Yes, you do know me,' she agreed equably. 'We've always been good friends and we always will be, no matter what. Although I can tell you're having a hard time feeling friendly just now. I'm sorry about that. The trip will be wonderful, though. Imagine, China! The great wall!'

How funny, Gen thought, that she had gone to England to think things over and now he was off to China for pretty much the same reason. They could spend years alternating trips to think things over, interspersed by brief disputatious get-togethers to supply new food for thought while apart.

Finally the conversation ended.

For some reason a sentence leapt into Gen's mind as

70

they said goodbye: 'I'm proud to be able to help in so grand a work.' Who was that? William Walker the diver, that's who. And that's what he said to the King. I wish I was engaged in some grand work. It would be so satisfying. So nice, also, to have a king to please. All these matters of the heart were so trying. William Walker, nobly slogging away – she thought enviously of his daily descent into the murky waters beneath the cathedral – he makes me feel so frivolous.

Meanwhile she was dialling Carl's number.

'Hello? His voice.

'This is Genevieve,' she said shyly. No response. 'I'm sorry I didn't call sooner. Just now I was thinking about William Walker the diver. He makes me feel so useless somehow.'

'It's a strange reason to call, because you feel useless. I don't believe anyone's called me because of that before.'

Genevieve smiled. Her heart flooded with warmth and began thudding as if one of those old steam radiators had been turned on inside her, banging away and warming her. 'Carl, how are you? I heard you were in hospital. I'm so sorry.'

'Did you hear why?' He sounded very subdued.

'Yes, I did. Are you all right now?'

'Why did you throw my roses into the water?'

'How could you possibly know that?'

'Tell me why you did it. I feel so hurt.' (In her whole life Gen had never heard a man say he felt hurt. It was very winning.) 'Give me a good explanation. You can lie.'

'It was horrible of me to have done such a thing. It's a long story why I did it but it had nothing to do with how beautiful they were or how very pleased I was to get them. Actually, I recovered most of them and enjoyed them for almost a week. Do forgive me if you can.'

'How gracefully said.' His voice was honestly admiring. 'I hardly noticed that you evaded my question entirely. I do forgive you.' His voice, enlivened now, continued enthusiastically, 'Did you by any chance press one of the

71

roses in a book in a fit of sentimentality and remorse?'

The vanity of the man! It wasn't enough that she'd recovered them and enjoyed them and was sorry. Here was a man who would always want more. It didn't occur to me, she would have liked to respond drily, but it had occurred to her and she had pressed one but he would *never* know. She did not reply, hoping he would think she did not deign to.

'How is your running?' he asked, after a small silence.

'How kind of you to ask. It's rather poorly, actually. But I'm coming back. And your music?'

'The same. I'm feeling like you. I wish I could do something more important. Save a cathedral. Or a world.'

'Why do you call yourself GEN?'

She realized she'd been saving up a million questions. And that she was very happy to hear his voice, his dear voice.

'Because all the great and meaningful words begin with Gen. Genius, genitals, generate, gentle, genuine. And they all apply to me.'

'What about gendarme?'

They laughed. What a good sound, she thought. Voices combined in joy.

'I'm so happy to hear your voice, your laugh,' he said. 'When shall we meet? Where?'

'Well. . .'

'Yes, a well is as good a place as any. We can go down together in a bucket. Shall I come right over?'

'No.' Gen felt alarmed. She wasn't quite ready for the onslaught of his typhoon-like personality.

'I have to come to Sausalito anyway. To buy a boat. A yacht, actually.'

Gen smiled to herself.

'You don't believe me.'

'I believe you. But why don't we meet tomorrow? Would you like to come here for a little supper? At six?'

'Yes.'

'I'll give you directions,' she said, and did, and said

goodbye.

As she replaced the receiver, she saw a man coming down her gangplank. He wore white rugby shorts and an Hawaiian shirt, faded from years of sun, green vines merging into purple blossoms, red sailing boats and sunsets. He was built close to the ground but it was more his presence that made you feel he could never be knocked off balance by anything or anyone. His face was open and handsome and friendly. He looked like a male version of her friend Sally. 'Hi,' he said. 'I'm Ricardo Luz, a friend of Carl Knight's.'

4

'Welcome aboard,' she said. 'I was just going to make some coffee. Would you like a cup?'

'Yes, please. Black. What a nice place!'

'Thank you.' Gen smiled with pleasure.

'It's so . . . cosy.'

'Yes, my husband was an architect and everything we had was so beautifully designed it was brutal. All leather and brass and stark white walls. When I finally got this place of my own I couldn't wait to get braided rugs and lamps with shades and the wing chair I'd always longed for with a little needlepoint footstool. The trouble is I spend my whole time apologizing for how cute it is.' She looked around. 'At least I didn't put on floral wallpaper. But only because I worried about the dampness.' She laughed.

'And you don't have collections of china animals,' he said approvingly.

'What is your place like?' She handed him a steaming mug.

'For now I just rent a couple of rooms in Carl's house. I suppose my place, when I get one, will be Mexican. White

73

stucco outside and lots of colours inside. Chickens in the garden, and probably a pig. Lots of kids.'

'Are your parents both Mexican?'

'Yes. I'm from a village near Guadalajara.'

'Is it hard to be a blond Mexican?'

'Sometimes, yes.'

Gen sugared her mug and he followed her to the tiny deck off her bedroom where two director's chairs and a straw table allowed them to sit overlooking the water.

'This is very old-world of me,' Rick said. 'I've come to speak for my friend and to melt your frosty heart. Mostly because I feel I've meddled and messed things up between you. You see' – he sat and put his feet up on the railing – 'Carl went into hospital the day you got back. When I came over here to tell you why he couldn't be reached, I arrived just as you were throwing out his roses. I went back and told Carl to forget you. It plunged him into a fit of gloom from which he has not yet emerged. I decided I'd been hasty, that I should hear your side, so here I am.'

'Thank you. I'm glad. But, as it turns out, I talked to Carl only minutes ago. I'd only just heard he'd been in hospital.'

'So much for subterfuge. Did you hear why?'

'Yes. My fiancé found out about it. He's very big in the medical community. I imagine he hoped to put me off Carl completely, but it only made me feel concerned for him. So I called.'

'He almost died.' Rick choked a little. 'He calls himself an occasional user, says he won't do it again. I don't know . . . What can you do?'

They sat comfortably, like old friends.

'What about the roses?'

Genevieve was silent.

'I know. You think it's none of my business. But it is. I've made it my business. Even if everything's OK now with Carl, I want to understand.'

'When I got back from the airport with my fiancé, Jim Lasky, the roses were here. Jim didn't mind. He doesn't

74

have a jealous nature. But we . . . were falling out in any
case. My daughter is in love with a Ugandan and it turns
out that Jim . . .' Gen sighed.

'Doesn't want a black in the family.'

'Yes. So, I told him . . . I guess I told him I didn't want
to marry him if that was the case. We had some words,
then he left, with a last angry glance at the roses, as if to
say he knew the real reason for all this – which is why I
threw them away. To prove to myself that my motives
were decent. It wasn't fair to Carl.'

'So, what about Carl? How do you feel about him?'

'I hardly know him. I've only seen him twice. I like him.
I'm flattered by his attention. But the whole thing's crazy.
I'm much too old for him. Still, I have to admit he makes
my heart pound. He has great force, great magic.'

'Yes, he does.' Rick appeared satisfied. 'Any more
coffee?'

'Help yourself.'

He whiled away another half hour with her, chatting
aimlessly, then took his leave.

As he was walking along the dock, he ran into Carl.

'Rick! What are you doing here? I come to spy on Gen
and I find you coming from her door. What is the meaning
of this, sir?'

'I came to speak for you. I figured I'd fucked it all up by
telling you about the roses so I thought I'd come and see
what's what.'

'This smacks of Cyrano de Bergerac to me. You'll do
the speaking and then she'll fall in love with you instead of
me. You, the handsome one! While I, the poet with the
ugly mug, who really loves her . . .'

'You're getting it all confused. Roxanne never loved
Cyrano the whole time.'

'She did too. At the end when he was dying and she
realized all the words she'd loved from Justin or Christian
or whatever his name was (it's the ugly men's names

which endure) were really Cyrano's! If you're going to speak for me you shouldn't be handsome too. Well, what did she say? Does she love me at all?'

'She's crazy about you. She explained about the roses and how she's cooling it with her fiancé and da di da di da.' Rick waved his hands. 'No problem.'

'So my only problem is you. Admit that you love her too.'

'You asshole. I think you really want me to be in love with her just to make it more interesting for you. You're nuts.'

'I want you to sleep with her for me. I know that you're better in bed than I am. I can tell by your blond hair and your muscles and your gross self-confidence that really amounts to insufferable arrogance. They did it in the old days. We just need a black, moonless night so she won't see it isn't me. Just the first time to make a good impression and set the standard of excellence. Then I'll take it from there. Don't be too kinky. This sort of thing was done all the time by the Knights of the Round Table. They'd take each other's place when one felt he couldn't get it up after a long day's chivalry. What do you say?'

'I'd say you're jumping the gun. She's not ready to go to bed with you.'

'That's true, but I've decided to start worrying about it now. It's never too soon to get anxious. I wish I knew if you really came here for my sake or for yours. I don't know whether to feel jealous or excited. And the trouble is I daren't antagonize you in case you leave the band. You're really what holds it up. And holds me up.' Carl wrung his hands. 'I need you but I don't *know* you.'

'You don't have to. But come back with me now. Don't spy on Genevieve. No sense antagonizing her as well as me.'

'You're right. This wooing is a tricky business. At any moment one can make a fatally wrong move and antagonize the hell out of the wooee. Let's go and buy a yacht. On the phone I told Gen I was coming over here to buy one, so

76

I'd better. Got any ideas? Will it take me long to learn to sail?'

'You could pick up the rudiments in a year and a half.'

'Then I'd better buy a skipper, too.'

'And a maintenance man. I can't see you over here every weekend scraping barnacles off the bottom.'

'What are barnacles?'

5

'Is that blond fellow the one who sent you the roses?' Ben asked an hour later. 'I feel a proprietary interest since I rescued them for you.'

'No.' Gen wondered if there was going to be any end to the roses business. She was on Ben's houseboat cutting his hair. An old pot-bellied wood-burning stove stood next to a large television. Two beds, an armchair, and a round oak table with four straight-backed chairs, were scattered about on oriental carpets. The living-room, galley and bedroom were all one room, his houseboat being more boat than house and having no pretensions towards either.

'Don't kid me. I saw you with him on your deck. You looked pretty chummy. Something's cooking there, I can tell.' Ben had found her affair with Jim very boring and longed for Gen's livelier days of the five lovers, some of whom got a second go around.

'I'm going to see the new one tomorrow night,' she said, so Ben wouldn't think she was holding out on him and not being neighbourly. In any case, here on the pier, her life was an open book.

'Well, who's the blond one, then?' Ben asked, a little querulously, she thought.

Gen felt a little querulous herself at having to refer to them as 'the new one' and 'the blond fellow', so she said,

'Rick. He's a friend of the new one, whose name is Carl. I told Rick you saved the roses so that I was able to enjoy them.' Actually they've given me more trouble than enjoyment, she thought. I'm beginning to hate those roses.

'Well, now, this fellow Rick, he's the blond one, right?'

'Right.' She wondered if Ben was purposely trying to infuriate her.

'You've so many I can't keep them straight. Jim's the old fellow . . .'

'He's thirty years younger than you, if that's old.'

'Don't cut it too short on top. I like it long up there but short around the ears.'

There wasn't much on top to be left long, but Gen pretended there were more of the fine white hairs than she could handle.

'Rick was asking me directions to your houseboat just as you were tossing the roses overboard, but he didn't come over.'

'That's enough about me. What about your love life? When's your sister-in-law coming?'

'Well, heck, I keep putting her off. I thought I was going to be so lonely when Mary passed away but I'm not. Feels like she's still here with me. Fifty years we were together. Fifty years of heaven. I just can't imagine someone else stepping in and taking over. Wouldn't seem right. Pretty close quarters here, too, although she's used to that since she lives in a trailer now. But, you know, Gen, when I come home each day and step through the door, I always say, "Hi, Mary, I'm home," because, well, it just seems like she's still here. "I got some fish for dinner," I say. I always bring two fish. She's been gone almost a year and I still bring two fish.'

Gen felt her nose get prickly and her eyes fill with tears.

'What do you think, Gen?'

'I don't know. It's tricky.' Gen thought that at any age the only reason to live with someone was for love of them. Why should it be different for Ben? It wasn't as if he were all alone in the country, or the city. They were a close-knit community, a village. 'Twenty years ago I'd have defined love as being willing to die for a man. Now I'd define it as being willing to live with one.' She paused, thoughtful. 'But you're looking for companionship, not love. It would be nice for you to have someone, but . . . I guess it would depend a lot on what she was like.'

'She's nice enough. But you never really know until you live with someone.'

'I haven't lived with a man for so long, I've forgotten how.'

'Well, you had a bad first experience. Takes a while to get over that.'

'Five years?'

'I think you and that blond fellow are going to get on just fine.'

Gen could tell Ben was going to be stubborn about Rick's being the new one. Only time would disabuse him.

'And don't you worry about the age difference. Mary was older than me and it never mattered except that she died first.'

'Was she older?' Gen was thrilled. She realized she needed a lot of encouragement about the 'age difference'. 'How much older?'

'Year and a half.'

'Oh.'

'When I married for the second time, all my friends told me to take a young bride – ten, twenty years younger. That way I could still have a family and she could look after me when I got old. Never mind that, I said. It's Mary I love.'

'Tell me, Ben, what do you think about a woman marrying a man who's ten or twenty years younger?'

'That's different. Not suitable, somehow. No, that wouldn't be right.'

Gen nodded gravely. 'I don't think it's right either. I'm surprised there isn't a law against it. I'm surprised they don't just throw a woman in jail for even looking at a

79

younger man.'

'My, my, pretty touchy.'

'It's just another of society's asinine prejudices.' She removed the towel from his shoulders, carried it to the door, and gave it a shake. 'How did you like having to retire at sixty-five when you are as sharp as ever at eighty? To say it's wrong for someone to do something because they're a certain age is just incredible!' Her voice rose in outrage. 'And why should it *ever* be wrong to love someone?'

'Well, I was glad to retire at sixty-five. They just don't make dead bodies like they used to.'

Ben had been a pathologist. Gen laughed, forgetting her ire.

'Now if I cut open some corpse, like as not I'd find a plastic heart and an aluminium liver.' He turned his head this way and that before the mirror. 'Pretty good haircut.'

'Thanks. You can pay me with a glass of that great old port of yours.'

'I will. It'll soothe you. You're always getting mad at society. What did society ever do to you?'

'Nothing. Because I'm white, smart, unhandicapped, beautiful and young.'

'What would you hate most to be,' Ben asked, pouring out the ruby drink, 'black, stupid, handicapped, ugly or old?'

Gen didn't have to think. 'Handicapped,' she said.

'Well, I'm already old and ugly and gimpy. I guess most of all I'd hate to be stupid. Although it would be awful, really awful, to be black.'

'Why, your best friend, Arnold, is black!'

'That's how I know it's awful.'

6

En route to his dinner date with Gen, Carl stopped at a florist's on Chestnut street and fell into a quandary. He didn't think roses would be a good choice after the unfortunate incident of the yellow ones, but he didn't want to go to something more exotic and seem to be trying to impress. Mixed bouquets were common. A plant was cumbersome and put the burden of eternal care on the recipient. In the end, he bought a bunch of white daisies. They were innocent and sweet. She would be touched.

She was touched. She accepted the daisies with a blush and a smile, saying, 'Let me put them in water at once,' bustling away from him and the awkwardness of their meeting.

'What an amazing place to live,' he said, appalled. 'It's so tiny.'

'It's disgustingly cute,' Gen apologized, wishing, as usual, that she hadn't. 'I tried to fight the cosiness but finally crumbled and gave in to the force of its adorable personality.'

'Which is really your adorable personality.'

Gen looked dismayed, 'Oh, dear, do you think so? I like to picture myself as somewhat wicked.' She thrust the daisies into a mayonnaise jar, fluffed them out, and set them on the table. 'If only I'd killed my husband as I meant to years ago, then I would be wicked. Well' – she gestured around her – 'at least I didn't name it *Bide a Wee*.'

'I've always wanted a house called *Loiter Longer*,' said Carl. 'You may have the name if you like.'

'I do like! *Loiter Longer* it is! I only wish I could say it with your accent.'

Carl was dressed all in white for the new nautical period he'd entered the day before. He who had been an indoor

81

person most of his life, a night person, was now all enthusiasm for the world of water and weather.

Gen brought him a bottle of wine and a corkscrew and he bungled it, breaking, not pulling, the cork. He dribbled the wine into the glasses through the crumbling cork. They were both nervous of each other, began speaking at the same time, stopped and urged the other, hectically, to go on. Even with the deck door wide open to the water, Carl felt cramped and confined. He hated this houseboat. His house in San Francisco, as in London, was gigantic. He wished they were there for this first evening, or that they had gone out. Maybe he should have kissed her at once, then there would not be this intolerable tension. There was no way to sit without seeming much too close to each other; at the same time, he could not move around as he talked, as was his wont, without falling into the water.

'Shall we go for a walk along the pier?' she asked, sensitive to his unrest. 'You might like to see some of the other houseboats.'

'Yes. Can we take our wine glasses with us?'

'Sure. Nothing surprises anyone around here.'

They strolled along, up and down the different piers. The water was turning lighter and lighter blue with the end of the day. Gen pointed out the different boats, telling stories, greeting members of the community, and Carl desperately wished they were back in the houseboat, alone. He felt as if he were on parade. He felt she was trying to amuse him and failing wretchedly, that she didn't know what to do with him, didn't like him. His white trousers and shirt and sweater seemed to blaze away, a walking searchlight, an ad for his washing powder. Every other man he saw was wearing faded jeans, mute and mellow, one with the water and sky, while he stood out like a polar bear.

Suddenly, in an agony of recollection, he thought of the daisies and wondered if she thought he'd chosen them to co-ordinate with his outfit. How incredibly stupid he must have looked on her doorstep, or door plank, rather, all draped in white with daisies to match. And the mess with the cork, followed by his sudden attack of claustrophobia, which must have been blatantly obvious or she wouldn't have suggested this hideous death march along the piers. Oh, how he wished he could begin the evening again, with roses, normal clothes, aplomb.

'Could we go back now?' he asked, rather pitifully.

'Of course, I'm sorry. We have walked a long way. I forget, being a runner, that others aren't.'

'Maybe we could get a taxi?'

She laughed. 'It's not that far. We've been going in circles really. We'll be back in no time.'

They were.

'Do you think it's too soon to become lovers?' he asked when he had refilled their glasses.

'Yes I do,' she said positively.

'It's true we haven't eaten yet. Maybe after dinner?'

'No, I think that's too soon too.'

'But we will be lovers, won't we? That's a foregone conclusion, isn't it?'

'I . . .'

He embraced her. 'Please just tell me we will and then I can relax.'

'It does seem to have a certain inevitableness about it.'

'Need you sound so doomed?'

'I'm not ready, Carl,' she said seriously. 'It's too soon even to be talking about it. We don't know each other at all. We simply have to wait.'

'Well, we'll definitely wait until after dinner.'

They laughed.

'Once we sat down to dinner, we relaxed.'

Gen shouted this information to Sally the next morning, over the noise of traffic, wind, fog horns and sandblasting. The Golden Gate was a great bridge to look at but absolute hell to run across.

She and Sally had taken the Sausalito ferry to the Ferry

Building in San Francisco and were running back to Sausalito. Now, having already traversed the Embarcadero, Fisherman's Wharf, Fort Mason, the Marina Green and the Embankment, they were on the Golden Gate bridge, hightailing it to Marin County.

Gen decided to wait until they had broken through the fog and out of the traffic before continuing her story. She took it up again when they were running the hill up to Alexander avenue from Fort Baker, where they could be abreast.

'And did you become lovers after dinner?' Sally asked.

'No,' Gen said honestly for, as it turned out, they'd become lovers before dinner, simply fallen into each other's arms without another word as if they'd been programmed, although her every instinct had cautioned her not to succumb for weeks, if ever. Afterwards Carl said it was he who had succumbed and that she, in the classical tradition of older women, had seduced him.

But she did not mention this. She had not fully registered it herself. On the run so far, she had told Sally of her reunion with Carl and how Rick had come round to check her out first. She had said nothing about the heroin overdose. She did not want to prejudice (that word again) her friend against Carl. Sally was prejudiced against anyone who smoked cigarettes, ate meat, took sugar in his coffee — even caffeine in his coffee! And here was Carl, mainlining! It would be bad enough when Sally saw he didn't have any muscular definition. Gen felt a little prejudice in that direction herself. But his forearms and hands were lovely. And he was slender.

She wondered how many of her friends and loved ones were going to approve of Carl for her. Even Ben seemed to have his heart set on 'the blond fellow'. Jim and Laura certainly were dead set against him.

And she herself had her doubts. 'It's hard to see how we could combine our lives successfully, if it ever came to that,' she said. 'Here I've striven for the simple life which all turns around my running, and he's out in the great

84

world giving concerts. He's living life on the fast lane and I'm on the bike path.'

'Or out on the marsh looking at a cattail,' said Sally, for Gen was one of the few serious runners who would stop in the middle of a timed run to look at a bird or flower. It made running with her exasperating at times.

When they were back at Gen's houseboat, stretching, Sally in the plough position, Gen doing hurdlers, Sally said, 'It pretty much sounds to me as if you've given up all idea of Jim.'

'I think I have. I didn't love him enough. Maybe I was trying, at the last minute, to commit myself to a sensible, secure, upright existence. Now I've decided to throw myself wholeheartedly into the life I love – living each day with no thought for the future or of how I'll feel when the present becomes the past. I spent twenty years being a good mother including fifteen years as an aggrieved wife and ten interminable ones as a sullen secretary. Now, for three years I've lived in absolute freedom and selfishness and it's growing on me. I'm getting good at it. It takes a while to learn how to be imprudent – especially when you begin as late as I have.' She smiled at Sally. 'I'm so glad you're doing what you want to do right from the start. It hasn't been easy for you either.'

'What is your aim in life now?' Sally asked.

'I'm going to disappoint you. It isn't a thirty-four minute ten K or a sub-five mile. My aim, instead, is to be aimless. I'd like to love a man as well as I've loved Laura, to keep up my running discipline but let go of the laurels, to learn how to live unwisely and so, in time, grow wise.'

'That sounds good,' said Sally. 'Me, I'll content myself with breaking two-thirty in the marathon and having my own animal hospital.'

Sally was a vet. She had taken pre-med in college to please her doctor father. When she told him she was going on, not to Harvard medical school, but to UC Davis, he cut her off without a penny. It had taken her many years to get her DVM, working to support her studies and her running. Now, with the death of her mother, there had been a rapprochement with her father and he was going to set her up in practice.

They concluded their stretching and tucked in to French toast made with sourdough bread, Gen washing it down with coffee, Sally with red mint tea.

Later Gen walked over to the day care centre for tiny tots where she volunteered her time three days a week. After her night of love, her good run and talk with Sally, the tasty breakfast, she felt on top of the world. She felt blessed. She thought, all I could wish for Laura in life is . . . is this!

This, and lots of children!

7

'I want to give you a car,' Carl said.

'I can't afford one,' said Gen, bringing him coffee in bed. For the first time in almost two weeks together as lovers, he'd consented to stay on *Loiter Longer*.

'That's why I want to give you one.'

'But the upkeep, insurance, gas. I live on eight thousand a year. It's tricky. And I don't need a car.' She got back into bed beside him, plumping the pillows behind so she could sit up.

'Eight thousand a year! I spend that in a week.'

'You do not!' Gen laughed.

'But, seriously, Gen, it would make life much simpler. Your running to the city to see me isn't practical. And you're so sweaty when you arrive.'

'I bike there, too.'

'But that still takes almost an hour. And you're still sweaty. Would you please ask those gulls to be quiet?' From the bed they could see a festival of seagulls careering about the surface of the water.

86

'Some herring must have got confused and come into the bay. Actually they're pretty smart. If the fishermen followed them in their boats, they'd all go aground.'

'If I needed you instantly,' Carl persisted, 'a car would have you at my door in fifteen minutes. And you'd look so pretty!'

Gen always arrived at his house very sweaty, it was true. She would shower and, like as not, put on some of Carl's clothes. The other women around the house, girl-friends of his musicians, were done up in mascara and silks. Not to mention how young they were . . .

It made her feel bad to hear him say it. She hung her head.

'Another alternative is that you could move in with me.'

'It's early days to be thinking of that. We still don't really know each other.'

'That continues to be your theme song. You said it in Laura's bedsit. You'll be saying it in our coffin-for-two, fifty years hence.'

'Anyhow, Laura's about to arrive. She's going to spend some time here with me, then with her father in San Francisco, then join Monti in New York.'

'Why are you looking hurt?'

Gen smiled. It was wonderful how available Carl was, how tuned in to each other they were. They did not play any games. They spoke their minds.

'I feel as if you're trying to change me. I want you to take me as I am.'

'I'm not asking you to stop running. I'm proud of your running even though I find your incredible fitness humil-iating. I'm only offering you transport, trying to make both our lives easier. It's often hard for me to come here. My life is seventeen times as busy as yours.'

'I know. I appreciate that. I wish you would come here more often than you do, though. I wish I felt you liked to come here.'

'You boat people are very amusing. I like this glimpse into squalid lives, but only occasionally.'

87

She hit him with a pillow. They wrestled and played and kissed and hugged and when all was serene again, she said, 'I feel you are comparing me with the other girls around your place and finding me wanting.'

'You are wanting. You're wanting a car.'

'What about . . . my age?'

They hadn't talked about it since their discussion in Laura's bedsit.

'I wish you were younger. I wish you were my age.'

She looked at him in amazement. He was deadly serious. He looked at her with pain in his eyes.

'Oh, Carl, sweetheart. I thought it was all right. I thought it didn't matter to you.'

'It does matter. It matters now because I love you. I want to marry you and have children with you. I want to have a life together. It's not just that you're so much older, it's that you have your own life and you're so bloody content with it. You don't need me, or marriage and children with me. You've done it. It's behind you. I feel cheated.'

'But I didn't think you wanted marriage and children. You have your life too, your music.'

'I have my music, but no life.'

She smiled, lightening up. 'You're just being a spoiled boy. You're only saying you want it because it's the one thing I can't give you. You didn't want it before, or you would have gone for some young childbearer and cabin-builder.'

'You bitch. How dare you understand me so perfectly? Are you going to let me give a car or not?'

'I'm not.'

'Well, fuck you. I've already bought it for you and it's out in the lot.'

'Oh, God,' she groaned. 'It's probably a BMW.'

'No, it's a Mercedes 450 SL.'

'No! Carl, it's too embarrassing. How could I hold my head up among the boat people?'

'I'm joking. It's not really a Mercedes. I wouldn't

88

subject you to such crass materialism. It's a Toyota.'

'I want a Mercedes!' she wailed.

They both fell to laughing again, to hugging, and kissing. 'Get on top of me,' he said excitedly. 'I want to see your rippling muscles as we make love.'

'I feel embarrassed on top, so exposed. I feel shy to have you see my orgasms.

'Don't worry, then. I won't give you any.'

'I wish,' she said seriously, 'I wish *you* would come more. Sometimes it seems to me that you're just bent on giving me pleasure, not taking enough for yourself.'

'What do you mean, I'm bent?'

She laughed.

'Do you really want me to have more pleasure?'

'Yes, of course!'

'Then let me put on some of your underwear.'

'Are you serious?' Gen felt shocked.

He smiled and entered her. She leaned over him, her hair filtering the sunlight and sealight, the flashing wings of seabirds. They kissed.

She wondered if he was serious. She hoped not. For one thing, her underwear was in shocking condition. She would have to buy new.

As if reading her thoughts, he said, 'Or a monkey suit. A monkey suit might do it.'

They stopped talking and dedicated themselves to their combining, which, thought Gen, was about the only time they were serious together. No, that wasn't true. They often talked seriously or were seriously quiet. Maybe it was the only time they were reverent together.

'You were fast asleep,' Carl said. 'You lay sprawled in that cramped little seat as if it were a sofa.'

'Your look awakened me.'

They lay in the completion of their embrace, reviewing the moment they met, their lips almost touching as they talked. It was about the fifth time they'd been through it.

89

They could recite it like a litany, but still sought for new impressions received at the time.

'I thought you were so pretty. Of course, the light wasn't good.'

'You couldn't tell how terribly, terribly old I was.'

'I still can't tell.'

'Your look lanced my sleep.'

'Then you put the blanket over your face, secluded yourself.'

He always sounded hurt at this point, as if he had been an old friend she was purposely avoiding.

'I still felt your eyes on me through the blanket. I waited for you to go away. Then I wished I had asked you to sit down with me so we could talk.'

'There wasn't an empty seat.'

'But I pretended there was and that I told you my life story, but then I fell back asleep before I could hear yours.'

'You still haven't told me your story.'

'You're the mystery man. I know nothing of your youth. I don't think you had one.'

'The next morning I learned that your eyes were brown. I'd imagined blue.'

'Tell me about sending Rick away.'

'He'd come for me in the Jaguar. I told him I was taking the tube. He said something suitably wry. He noticed you at once.'

'Then you got huffy with him.'

'I made it clear that you weren't just anyone. You were the incipient love of my life, no idle pick-up. An idle pick-up I would have taken in the car and she would have been thrilled. Whereas you hardly allowed me to come into the same tube carriage with you.'

'I was drawn to you, really, but at the same time fearful you would . . . would . . .'

'Impinge on your time. You are still afraid of that.' Suddenly Carl catapulted out of bed and began to walk agitatedly about. 'Why? Why? Why aren't you happy to

90

be with me every minute of the day? Why won't you live with me?'

'But, Carl, sweetheart . . .' She reached for him but he drew himself up haughtily, 'got huffy'.

'You won't even accept a car to facilitate your crossing.'

Gen laughed. 'Crossing sounds so funny,' she said. 'But it's true, there is a body of water between us. Still, I think you just said it because you're so cross.'

'I am not cross. I'm full of hate. I hate you with all my heart. Will you accept the car or not?'

'I will.'

8

Gen picked up Laura at the airport in her sky-blue convertible Mercedes.

'This is disgusting,' Laura said.

'Isn't it absolutely revolting,' Gen agreed tranquilly. 'Don't tell Monti. He thinks I'm a terrible capitalist as it is. I was so embarrassed about it at first that I never put the top down and wanted to drive around with a bag over my head. But then I came round. What the heck, I thought, relax and enjoy your luck. It's a super machine.' (All this 'coming round' had taken less than a day.) 'And look!' she added. 'It means I can come and meet you at the airport!'

'I could have taken the limo.'

'I know.'

'My mother, the kept woman.'

'Oh, come on!'

'And kept by a boy!'

'I don't care what you think or what anyone thinks. I'm happy. Carl is the most wonderful man I've ever known. He's sweet and affectionate and fun to be with. We laugh so much. And yet life isn't easy for him. He's quite compli-

cated and tormented. That's why I'm good for him. I'm so
simpleminded.'

'What about poor Jim?'

'Poor Jim is in China at some scientific congress.'

'Does he know?'

'He has a pretty good idea.'

'Does Carl want to marry you?'

'We haven't discussed it much. Laura, you loved it that
Jim wanted to marry me, but I didn't. It felt like a trap-
door shutting. I don't want to get married. I've been
married. There's no reason to marry unless one is going to
have children. It's different at my age. One wants different things.'

'Like what?'

'I just want to . . . be.'

'But be what? You don't want to work, you don't want
to marry. You wrote that you've decided to stop racing. I
don't get it. It makes me worried.'

'I told you about the revelation I had while running
through London with Monti – that running was good in
itself. I have my American record, which makes me feel
good about myself, but I'm no longer possessed. One has
to be pretty singleminded, not to mention monomaniacal,
to maintain that level of fitness – just as Carl has to be
possessed to be the artist he is. I want to expand my being
. . . by being. Anyhow' – Gen felt she was getting too
heavy, too defensive – 'I want you to think about your life,
which is all ahead of you. Don't worry about me. I'm
happy.'

'You do look happy. I'm sorry, Mom. I don't know why
I'm getting at you. It's just that you'd finally achieved the
life you wanted to lead – pure and ascetic, really, simple
and disciplined – and it just seems defiled now by this
Mercedes.'

'True, but after much thought I've decided I can live an
ascetic life that includes a forty-thousand-dollar
vehicle. I did a lot of soul-searching, and my soul lost. I
now have a simple life with a much broader reach, so to

92

speak. But enough of your wayward mother. Tell me about Poland.'

'I will later. All I can say now is that going there really makes me appreciate America. Look! There's the bridge. Oh, it's so beautiful. It really is so great to be home.'

'About ten of your old friends have called and are wild to see you.'

'Good. How's Sally?'

'Terrific. She's gearing up to win the San Francisco marathon, although she'll have a little competition in Alison Roe.'

'And Ben?'

'In a way he's my best friend of all. We have such good talks. But now I have a new friend, Rick Luz.'

'The guitarist?'

'Yes. He's Carl best friend and a wonderful guy. Quiet, serious.'

'Monti thinks he's the best guitarist around. He says Carl is a great entertainer, a truly original artist, but for pure musicianship and emotional depth Rick is in another sphere.'

'I don't know enough about music to tell. Rick is a blond Mexican. People don't think of him as third world but he's deeply Hispanic. He lives simply, because he sends all his money home so his enormous family can be housed, fed and educated. It sounds as if his whole home town is related to him. It's a kept town, as I'm a kept woman. But I think even if he didn't do that he'd live austerely. Carl marvels at his lifestyle, can't understand it.'

'He sounds more your type than Carl.'

'Please, Laura, open your mind to Carl. I love him.'

'I don't trust him. I don't want you to get hurt.'

'Then you might as well tell me you don't want me to love and don't want me to feel.'

'I don't want you to love,' said Laura. 'I don't want you to feel.'

Gen sighed. 'When will you go to your father's?'

93

'He's away now, so it won't be for another week.'

They drove the last five miles silently. Gen found herself thinking about her ex-husband, and the story she had not yet told Carl. Or anyone.

When she was twenty and pregnant with Laura, Ted Randall married her despite the fact that he knew it was not his child she carried. He did her that unpardonable kindness. And she had to be grateful. Part of the deal was that Laura would never know he was not her real father. They moved straight away from the east coast to San Francisco, to begin their life together away from the tightly-knit society they had both been raised in.

It was too bad. Now Gen looked about and saw how easily an unmarried woman could have a child with no stigma attached to her or the child. People lived together and had children, married or not. And if a man wanted to live with a man he could do that too without losing his place in business or society.

When Jim's sperm fertilized Gen's egg, he was already married with two little boys so couldn't marry her. When she moved to San Francisco, Jim went to Washington with his family to work for NIH. Years later, when he was offered the job of heading the lab at the Bay Area Medical Center, he accepted and wasn't long in tracking down Gen and Laura and making himself important in their lives. Gen was divorced by then but living celibately. He was still married. When Laura went east to college, Gen moved to Sausalito. A couple of years after that, Jim's wife died and, after a suitable mourning period, he began wooing Gen in earnest. By then she had experienced the five lovers and was not overwhelmed, did not seem to have been waiting for him all these years.

It was probably natural that Gen and Jim's friendship should turn again to love now they were both free. Maybe she never had stopped loving him. But she couldn't get rid of the feeling that he was 'making things right'. At last.

Doing for her and Laura what he'd been unable to do when they needed him. But it was too late! There was nothing to be made right at this point – except in his own heart. Also, Gen felt it was Laura he was marrying in a way, wanting to secure her as a daughter. As if it were really Laura he loved, not Gen. Laura was his blood.

From the start his insistence on marrying had made Gen uncomfortable. It was why she had wanted to get away to England to think. Maybe now she was seizing on Carl so as not to succumb to Jim. And seizing on the fact of Jim's prejudice.

Off the hook! She had to admit it felt good.

Or could it be that she was revelling in refusing Jim because, when she desperately loved and needed him, he had failed her?

No, she didn't think it was that. It would not be in her character to feel vengeful. Would it? Anyhow, it was always her husband, Ted, she had hated for marrying her, instead of Jim for not. Hate transference? If so, the more she dwelt on it, the more she felt a glimmer of hate transferring back to Jim, as if at last it had found its rightful place. This, also, felt good.

Curious that, until now, she had never examined her feelings in terms of her history. It takes so long to understand one's behaviour, to gain perspective.

She and Ted Randall had been friends since grade school. Their parents hoped they would marry – but they liked each other anyway.

No one knew of her love affair with Jim Lasky. When Ted asked her to marry him he didn't know either.

She had told him, in floods of tears, tears of shame and hurt, and of sorrow at hurting him, that she was in love with another man and pregnant by him.

Ted, stricken, went away, but returned in a few days saying he still wanted to marry her and would raise the child as his own.

And so it was arranged. She tried to love him, pretended to, and he, realizing this in time, had to pretend

95

not to love her. The nicer he was to her, the worse she felt, and so, in self-defence, she began to hate him, in order to have a reason to break free.

Gen was still thinking all this as they arrived in Sausalito and Laura settled into *Loiter Longer*. She could not discuss it with her daughter, but she could say, 'Laura, I am so glad of your love for Monti. Marriage is difficult, and your marriage will be more difficult than most, but where there's love anything can be overcome. Without it — torture!'

'Torture?' Laura laughed. 'Surely not.'

Gen was about to explain when she looked up and saw Carl, just passing Ben's house next door. 'Oh, here comes Carl! I didn't expect him.' She felt awash with anxiety, as if somebody had sprayed her with it, turned on her with a hose that peppered every particle of her skin with trouble so she had to shudder it away as a horse would flies.

She hadn't expected him. In fact, she had particularly said to him that she wanted the afternoon alone with Laura and would see him in the evening.

Carl hadn't expected to come. But he found himself in Sausalito, finalizing the purchase of the yacht, and naturally he wanted to celebrate by inviting Gen out for a sail. He'd also bought her a gift. 'A Nautalis machine,' he told Rick as they had a cup of coffee together at the Café Trieste. 'It's to build her upper body. As it is, she has to go all the way to Mill Valley high school to work out at some night class. This way, it's available to her all the time. It's important for a runner to have strong arms. One wouldn't think so, but it is. I want to encourage her. I'm such a selfish son of a bitch and I'm afraid she's giving up her racing for my sake. Do you think she'll be pleased?'

'Sure she will. Don't you think so?'

Carl thought a minute, then looked woeful. 'No,' he said. 'I'm afraid she'll just think it's another way of trying to keep her near me. Maybe it is. I hope not. I want to do

96

nice things for her that are selfless. It's hard. I'm so used to thinking of just me.'

Now Carl felt embarrassed that he'd burst in on them and that Gen looked so dismayed (the woman hadn't the least idea how to disguise her feelings) so he brazened it out, lying barefacedly, insinuating he thought she'd expected him. 'I'm sorry I'm late.'

'Late? But . . .'

He embraced her, kissed her, then held out his hand to Laura. 'Hello, Laura, welcome home.'

'Thanks,' said Laura, taking his hand.

Gen looked hopefully from one to the other. It's going to be all right, she thought.

'I had to stop and watch a breathtaking chess game between Ben and his friend, Arnold. Who would have thought that a boat person could play chess?'

'Boat person?' said Laura, shocked. 'How condescending.'

'He's just joking,' said Gen and desperately wished she hadn't. She feinted. 'Carl, would you like some . . . '

Laura interrupted, saying, 'I suppose you interfered with his game. Probably you stood over him and advised his every move.'

Now that really was an unnecessarily disagreeable thing to say, Gen thought.

'Of course!' Carl responded gaily.

'Ben hates people who do that,' Laura said scornfully.

'But you see, I am trying to alienate all your mother's friends. That way she'll have no one left but me.'

Now Gen was clasping her hands together, looking beseechingly from one to the other.

'It won't work. Mom is very loyal to her friends. You'll only end by losing her if you take that tack.'

'No, not at all. The more I am deplored by her loved ones, the more stoutly loyal she'll be to me. It's you who's on the wrong tack. You have to understand your mother's psychology.'

'Laura, *please* understand that Carl is joking. You

97

mustn't take him so seriously.'

'I know he's joking, but only because that's his style. He still means what he says.'

'She's right, I do, Gen, darling. All my jokes are only a smokescreen for my true malignancy which Laura has acutely penetrated.'

'Please! Both of you . . .' Now Gen was in acute misery.

'I'm sorry, Mom. I'm going to call my friends.' She took the phone to the bedroom and closed the door.

'Oh dear,' Gen said weakly.

'Here, have some brandy.' Carl rummaged in the cupboard for the Courvoisier he'd brought the other night. He poured some into a wine glass, not having yet bought her snifters.

'I haven't run yet.' She pushed it away.

Carl drank it at a gulp, gratefully – he needed it more than she did.

'Maybe I should go for a run now.' Her heart lightened at the thought. 'It would do me good. We really did plan to meet later, you know.'

'I know.' He looked desolate.

'I love you,' she said. They kissed each other.

'I wish I could come running with you. I want to be with you. I hate it even when you're in a different room from me. I could drive along beside you.'

'Not on the bike path you couldn't. Runners, walkers, bikers and birdwatchers would feel dispossessed.'

'I could bike along with you. Couldn't I?'

Gen entertained the notion and discarded it. 'I want to run fast and alone. I don't want a sociable run just now. But another time we could do that. Why don't you go and annoy Ben some more? I won't be long. Forty-five minutes.'

'I could go and sit on my yacht and mope. My yacht. *Encantada*, that is.'

'Did you buy it?'

'Yes, that's why I came over. I want to take you and Laura for a sail this evening.'

'How wonderful! May she invite friends?'

'By all means. It will heal the breach. Hmmm, that sounds quite nautical in itself. We've already set a precedent by talking about tacks . . .'

Watching her change into her running clothes, Carl grew excited and slipped down his trousers.

'No, no.' She smiled. 'Not with Laura in the next room and certainly not with my diaphragm in the next room. I'm going to have to get a new one. It's exhausted. It's experiencing rubber fatigue from the continuous wave action. Do you know you're insatiable?'

'Yes,' he said happily.

9

While Gen was running, Carl met Rick at *Encantada*, a sloop-rigged Bowman, forty-six, and the skipper sent them off to the ship-chandler for a water-pump impeller. The cashier was adorable, a pert and lively twenty-year-old. Carl flirted with her. Walking out with Rick, he said, 'She was cute.'

'Yeah,' said Rick indifferently.

'I think she likes me. I think she fell for me like a ton of bricks.'

Whenever Carl used Americanisms, Rick got edgy. He looked sideways at Carl and asked, 'So what?'

'So she's cute. I think I'll go back and ask her for her phone number.'

'Are you kidding?' Rick stopped and turned to him.

'No, I'm completely serious.'

Carl turned to go back to the store. Rick grabbed him and swung him round. His eyes flashed. Carl pulled away, saying, 'Don't hit me. Your hands! You'll hurt your hands!'

Rick let go and said angrily, 'What the hell's the matter

with you? You're happy with Gen. You love her. What do you want to mess around with that little twat for?'

'I'm getting too attached to Gen.'

'You're supposed to. That's what love is about, man.'

'No it isn't. I get dependent and start acting like a fool. She's so independent. If I see other women I'll be more in control.'

'You'll also lose Gen.'

'Maybe she'll understand. Maybe she won't mind.'

'She'll mind.'

Carl turned again to go back to the store.

'You're being completely self-destructive. You know that, don't you?'

'It's doomed anyway. The whole thing is doomed. How do I know she won't go back to this Jim when he gets back from goddamn China? What do I know about their history, how deep their friendship goes? Ours is totally shallow. And Laura hates me.'

'What do you want? Instant dimension? It takes time to get to know someone and develop a history together. You'll never do it this way. You'll just hurt her horribly – and yourself. This is the time to be building trust.'

'Mind your own damn business,' Carl said. He went into the store. He waited until the girl had finished dealing with a diver who was arranging for some boat bottom to be cleaned. When the diver left, she turned to him. 'Remember me?' he asked.

'You were just in here a minute ago.'

'My name is Carl. What's yours?'

'Dotty.'

'Well, Dotty, would you like to come sailing with us this evening? We're leaving in about an hour.'

'Sure,' she said. 'That would be nice.'

Gen had a good run. It was a hot afternoon and the sweat pouring from her body, exertion's watery release, seemed a release for her psyche too, a stretching out. Her whole

100

body seemed to be making an escape. She hurtled down the bike path to Mill Valley, Mount Tamalpais leaping towards her.

Returning to Sausalito, she eased up and cruised on in, slowing to a walk when she reached the piers. Ben was just putting the chess pieces back in the box. He gave her a message from Carl: to meet him on his yacht at five. Then he said, 'Pearl's coming.'

'Pearl?'

'My sister-in-law. She's due in tomorrow morning.'

'Oh my goodness. How exciting! It's really happening.' Gen felt her heart sink. Change, she thought. How we all hate change, resist it, feel threatened by it. I do, anyhow. 'We must have a party to welcome her.'

'Let's just take it easy and see. Sort of ease her in and see how she likes it here.'

'He means see how she likes him,' Arnold said. Arnold was enormous, easily three hundred pounds. Ben's boat seemed to tilt under his presence.

'How could she not love Ben?' Gen asked. 'She's such a lucky woman. I hope she knows how lucky.' (This direly, as if Gen would teach her if she didn't.)

'We'll tell her,' Arnold promised. 'We'll see that she finds out right away.'

Back on *Loiter Longer*, Gen slowly drank a cold Calistoga water with lime, standing on the deck, feeling happy. On her mirror, a note from Laura declared she was with her friends and would meet Gen at Carl's boat.

Gen showered, then dressed in Levis and a green turtle-neck jersey. Departing, she took extra sweaters just in case. Although it was a balmy evening, at any moment a summer fog could come weaselling in through the gate or pour effulgently over Wolfback Ridge.

She walked over to *Encantada*'s slip, feeling relaxed, looking forward to the evening ahead.

'Welcome aboard,' cried Rick.

'Oh, how beautiful it is!' Gen had seen the boat when Carl was considering it, but now it was his she could really enthuse.

Carl introduced her to the skipper and a girl named Dotty, and then Laura arrived with three friends, two of whom had boyfriends with them.

They motored away from the slip and set sail, heading for Raccoon Strait.

Both Rick and Dotty knew their way around a sailing craft, and Gen remembered some moves from her days of small-boat racing in Marblehead twenty-five years before. Carl wasn't handy but he was curious. He wanted to know the name of everything and what to do with it and why. He wanted to know about winds and navigating by the stars. He wanted to take the tiller, did, and grinned like a kid when he got the feel of it. Gen loved watching him.

It was a nice time all in all, Gen thought. A pretty evening, just enough breeze. They anchored off Angel Island and had a picnic supper. Laura chattered with her friends, three of whom were thrilled to be sailing with two of GEN. It seemed that GEN was a meeting place for lovers of rock, soul, reggae, punk, or jazz. They could dig GEN without being disloyal to their main music. (Although 'no one says dig any more', Laura informed her.) The girl, Dotty, seemed amazed, almost cowed, to learn that Carl and Rick were GEN and it made Genevieve wonder, in that case, who on earth Dotty was. Maybe a friend of the skipper.

She didn't have much opportunity to be alone with Carl, but she was able to tell him during supper, 'Ben's girlfriend is coming tomorrow. We're all agog to see her. Her arrival had been imminent for months but now she's really coming.'

'I can't understand your excitement over other people's lives.'

'Really?' That gave Gen pause. She couldn't imagine not being interested in other people's lives. Certainly in her friend's lives. But she recognized that Carl wasn't. He wasn't even interested in Rick. He never inquired into her

102

own life before she knew him, as if she only came into existence with their meeting. She thought this unusual. He lived for his music and for the moment. He simply could not be bothered with . . . well, gossip was what it came down to, she supposed. I'm just a low gossipmonger, she thought. But by telling Carl about Ben I'm able to release my anxiety about it. He's my best friend, my nearest neighbour. Now here comes this stranger into his life who will have first claim on him. That's what I'm really saying when I say we're all agog; I'm saying I'm scared.

'He's my dear friend . . .'

'Propinquity has made you friends. If either of you moved away, you probably wouldn't see each other,' Carl said, rather more sternly than was warranted, Gen thought, as if propinquity were a serious offence.

'Possibly, but we wouldn't stop caring about each other. Also, because of that propinquity, our doings do affect each other's lives.'

'You shouldn't let them.'

'But it's not a bad thing. It's nice. It's neighbourly.'

'I just think all this caring you have for others, for Laura, Ben, Sally, Jim, is love you could be giving me.'

Gen smiled. 'Love needn't be rationed. It's inexhaustible.'

'Then you wouldn't resent my loving other people?'

'Of course not!'

It was nine o'clock when the boat was berthed and all was once again shipshape. Carl and Gen were the last aboard.

'It was a splendid time. Thank you so much. Laura really enjoyed herself, I could tell. You were most hospitable.'

'That's good. Are you going?'

'Well . . . I was waiting for you.'

'I thought you'd want to spend the time with Laura now, since I broke up your afternoon with her.'

103

'Oh, I expect she's gone off with her pals. I'll see her in the morning. It's all right.'

'It's not quite all right, actually, since I've made other plans.'

'Other plans? Oh, you mean thinking I'd be with Laura. Well, that's all right, then.' She smiled. 'Could the plans include me?'

'Not very well. I'm meeting Dotty.'

'Dotty? You mean the girl who was on board with us? I don't understand.'

Carl was silent.

'You made a date with her?' Gen's voice quavered.

Carl began to speak but the words made no sense to Gen. They were distorted, scrambled, speeded up. Nevertheless, the facts became clear to her – Carl had made a date with another woman and it was all over with them. She began to tremble from head to foot, to feel disoriented and afraid. I've got to get away right now. She felt a blinding, animal surge of panic. Help!

'You're not even listening to me,' he said. 'What are you doing? Where are you going?'

'I've got to go now,' she said stupidly. (Help! Help!)

There was a space of water between the boat and the pier, glimmering darkly. She didn't see how, with her body shaking, she could make it across. She imagined herself exiting straight into the water, just stepping off the boat into the sea. Down she would go and that would be the last of her. She would sink like a stone.

'I've got to go now,' she repeated, hoping that she meant away, not under. The watery hurdle assumed mammoth proportions.

'Wait. I'll walk with you to your boat.'

'No, no – don't.'

She stepped and did not go into the water. She began walking away, holding herself rigidly so that she wouldn't fragment. She passed some people who said her name but she didn't see them. It was as if her eyeballs were turned around, looking inward, and locked, so that she just saw

104

the inside of her skull, which was empty. There was no brain. Only a cranial void.

All I hope, Gen thought, as she stumbled along the pier (stumbling because her body had gone from rigidity to flaccidity and she felt like a rag doll, limbs without bones, muscles or tendons, covered with skin of rag. If this feeling continued to obtain, she would never run again), is that Laura is not home. That's all I hope.

She still wanted to protect Carl. She did not want Laura's fears for her to appear to have been borne out. (I don't trust him. He'll hurt you.)

A tintinnabulation of voices greeted her from the boat. She paused, wondering if she should go to Ben's instead. Then the young people burst out of the door. Even in the night light, Laura took one look at her mother and exclaimed, 'Mom! What's wrong?'

Gen was afraid to trust her voice, feared an accompanying gush of tears.

The next thing she knew, Carl had grabbed her arm, was pushing her through the children to the door. 'We have to be alone,' he said. 'Let us through, please.'

How wonderful to be taken in hand – even by one's enemy.

10

Carl brought out the old Courvoisier again and poured them both a glass. 'How could you just walk away from me like that? Without even saying goodbye.' He glared. 'You just walked away. I felt so hurt.'

Expecting apologies, she was instead attacked. At first she was, as they say, speechless with surprise. Then the raggediness fell away and a cleansing anger cleared her mind. She became blue, twisted steel, one big bunch of rooted rheobars. 'You were hurt! You! When you, my

105

alleged lover, pick up a strange girl and invite her along on *our* evening. Flaunt her!' Heated, she flung off her sweater.

'I did not in the least flaunt her. You didn't even know I'd asked her aboard until the end.' As always he looked interested in her disrobing, hoped for more.

'Then you coolly tell me you have a late date with her. A date!'

'You were so rude to walk away like that. It's hard to believe you could be so unfeeling.'

'Rude! I was having a seizure.'

He was succeeding at throwing her on the defensive. It was the most unfair thing she'd ever heard of. She gulped the cognac, coughed. Her brain became searingly clear, scalpel sharp. She'd get the best of him yet.

Instead, she said beseechingly. 'Carl, tell me why you did it.'

'You said tonight on the boat that I could love other people, didn't you?'

A trap, she thought.

'Just as you love Ben and Jim and Laura . . .'

'I don't have sex with them.'

'Because you can't have sex with a man in China or with a man who's eighty. What's sex anyway?' Carl inquired rather savagely. 'What's sex got to do with love and loyalty?'

'Everything,' she said decisively.

'What does what I do with others or feel about others have to do with my feelings for you? Love is inexhaustible, you said. It can be spread about indefinitely.'

'If you started seeing Dotty, you would want to spend time with her.'

'As you want your time with Laura, your time to run.'

'That's different.'

'How is it different?'

They'd been standing close to each other, eyes locked, chins out, Carl occasionally waving his hands about, splashing cognac. Now Gen threw herself down on the couch, exhausted. 'Oh, Carl, you know it's different. You know in your heart it is. All this talk is intellectualizing, twisting facts. The heart tells you what's right. Feelings of utter misery, like mine now, tell you what's wrong.'

'I was miserable when you said you wanted to go running alone today. Go and annoy Ben, you said.'

'I'm sorry. I'm sorry I said that. But, Carl. Oh, my darling, everthing is so wonderful with us, so perfect. I can't bear to think that you need someone else, that I'm not enough for you. I'll be more considerate. I'll see my friends when you are rehearsing and practising. And I'll run then, too.'

I am making wild promises, she thought. I'm drunk.

He looked terribly pleased. He poured them more cognac and came and sat beside her. 'I've bought you a Nautalis machine so you can work out at my house. And some dumb-bells too. Now you won't have to go all the way to the high school to work out at night.'

Oh, lord, she thought. The idea of working out alone made her feel wretched. She loved the night class at Tam High where she joined a motley crew of men and women and circled around the machine, taking turns at the different weights, chatting and laughing and gossiping, a festival of muscle building, all fellow travellers on the great journey from puny to strong. There were shop girls, a teacher, a journalist, an accountant, a roofer, two other runners . . .

'Are you pleased?' Carl asked.

Gen took another giant gulp. Should she lie to him and say she was pleased? Should she begin to mar their communication, which was a great thing about their love, being as honest with each other as they knew how to be? Enter deceit, she thought, swinging its ugly head, all mouth, like a giant termite. Enter erosion.

'No,' she said, 'I'm not pleased.'

They both looked relieved. 'I didn't think you would be. But I got it just for you. All for you. For your arms, you know, so you can be stronger and faster. You're a beautiful runner. I watched you set off today. I watched until

107

you were out of sight.'

'I didn't mean to sound ungracious about the Nautalis.'

'I know.'

'Will you stay?' Gen asked, a little fearfully. He still might keep his date with Dotty, if there was a date.

'Yes.'

'I'm so glad.'

'You were terribly hurt, weren't you,' he asked as they got into bed.

'Yes. I felt as if my body was becoming a hundred and fifty years old before my very eyes. It felt like a piece of petrified wood.'

'That would be a hundred and fifty thousand years old . . .'

'And then like a rag doll.'

'Your metaphors are hopelessly confused. But never mind, I love you.' Carl sighed happily and took her tenderly into his arms.

Their love-making, even without the monkey-suit, grew better all the time. Gen loved to relive it afterwards. Tonight she said, 'I felt on the precipice, on the verge of orgasm but withholding it. The excitement was so intense, it was actually terror. It was the fear of falling . . . to my death. Then you took me to an even higher precipice and still I held back and all the time, subconsciously, I was waiting for you to fall with me. Then you did and we fell together and we fell and we fell and, astonishingly, did not die, and it was perfect.'

'Ummmm,' said Carl.

'You don't like to talk about it. Do I annoy you? Do I sound stupid?'

'You live too much in the past. All that orgasm business was minutes ago. Now I'm at peace.'

'But don't you feel we have returned from a great adventure? I do. My mind and body are still reverberating . . .'

But Carl's breathing told Gen he was sleeping, not reverberating. When he moved so that she was no longer

108

in his intensely loving grasp, she eased out of bed, put on a robe, and tiptoed to the living-room, softly closing the sliding door between.

Since Laura had planned to sleep in the double bed with her and now could not, she'd better make a comfortable place for her on the floor. Gen realized, as she pulled out a sleeping bag and found another pillow, that Carl had managed to intrude not only on her afternoon with Laura, and the evening, but also on the night. She wondered if he had somehow orchestrated the whole thing.

She shook her head. Imagine him arriving and saying, sorry I'm late, when she had not asked him to come at all! How outrageous he was. He probably bought the boat just so that he could invite them all for a sail – and only asked Dotty along so they would fight and make up.

No, surely not. Probably it all fell out by chance. But she wouldn't put it past him. He was impetuous and unaccountable, but also determined to have things his own way, sparing no expense to see that he did.

'Goodbye, you total angel.' Carl leaned over and gave her a kiss. He was fully dressed. It was early morning.

'Where are you going,' she asked drowsily. 'Let me make you some coffee.'

'No, I forbid you to move. I've decided to confound you by being considerate and getting out of here. I'll call you later. Sleep. Cheerio.'

He crept out. In the living-room he stumbled over Laura, who was stretched out in the middle of the floor in her sleeping bag. The curtains were drawn and it was dark.

'You kicked me,' Laura said. 'You purposely kicked me.'

'Are you kidding?' he whispered. 'Do you really believe that?'

'I'd believe anything after your act last night. Mom's so naïve she can't see what's going on. I think you're a

109

crumb.'

'Listen, if I'd meant to kick you, I'd have gone for your head.'

'Do you know that Mom has the American mile record for women over forty?'

This so surprised him that, quick as his mind was, Carl missed a beat. Then he said. 'Of course I know. I've listened to it. The sound track is terrible.'

She waggled her hand in the air and closed her eyes. Carl recognized the gesture. It meant he was being fanned, that he was too worthless to enter into a discussion with. He had a wild urge to pick her up, bag and all, and throw her into the water. But he knew he wasn't strong enough. Well, he was going to use the Nautalis machine he'd bought for Gen and get strong enough. At their next encounter, she'd quail before his outstanding musculature, his giant pectorals and washboard stomach. He'd be the world's first strong-man flautist.

He decided to make an effort since he hadn't made one so far. He squatted down and spoke into her ear. 'Look, Laura, I love your mother. I want to love you, too. Let's be friends.'

Laura opened her eyes and considered.

'I'm not a crumb. Really. Ask Rick if I'm a crumb. Ask Monti.'

'I just want you to be good to her,' she said, touchingly childlike.

'I'd do anything in the world for her. Anything! Ask me!'

'I'll think about it.' She turned over and shut her eyes.
A stand-off.

Carl made his way out of *Loiter Longer* and up the ramp to the pier. Ben was coming down it, carrying luggage. Behind him walked an upright, grey-haired little woman. Pearl, Carl remembered. She's come. But he was too excited about Gen's record to think about Pearl. Why had Gen never told him? 'Ben! Do you know that Gen's the fastest woman over forty in the whole country?'

110

Ben smiled. 'Well, I'm not surprised.'

'Here, let me give you a hand with those bags.'

'Thank you, Carl. I want you to meet Pearl Dedston.'

Pearl and Carl assessed each other. She had very sharp eyes. He rather thought that the lines around her mouth were from pursing her lips, not smiling. 'How do you do, Pearl.'

'You're GEN.'

'That's right,' he said, pleased that a woman her age should recognize him.

'My nephew has all your albums. That's how I know. He plays them night and day.' She covered her ears. 'Lordy!'

'I suppose you're not a musical person yourself,' Carl said stiffly.

She drew herself up. 'I know what I like.'

'I bet you do.'

'I beg you pardon?'

'I bet you do,' he said, so loudly that she shrank back.

'Take it easy, Carl.' Ben patted his shoulder.

'She insulted me. She referred to my music by covering her ears.'

Ben laughed. 'Sometimes people our age just hear the din in young people's music.'

'Din, eh? Maybe I should call myself DIN instead of GEN.'

'Maybe you should,' said Ben, still laughing. Pearl looked on disapprovingly. She knew what she liked and she didn't like laughter.

'Do you live here?' she asked, as if that would decide whether or not she did.

'No, but I'm a friend of Genevieve's.' He wished he'd said he was her lover.

'Why, Ben, that's the friend you wrote so much about. She sounded such a nice girl.'

'She is nice,' said Carl. 'That's why she likes me. In fact, she's so nice she'll probably even like you.'

He carried the luggage in as he promised, then fled.

111

Why do I bring out this hostility in everyone? he wondered. I never did before. Or maybe I did but I never noticed. I never cared. Now I care because these people are connected with Genevieve. These horrible, horrible people.

You are kind to the few people you care about, Aunt Fanny had said.

A few is quite a lot, really, he thought as he got into the white Jaguar. Three. Let's see, that would be Rick and Genevieve and who's the third? Me, I suppose. How could I forget my favourite? Gen and Rick and me. I'm going to be even kinder to us all. I'm going to overwhelm us with kindness and screw everyone else. Especially Pearl.

He started the engine and drove through Sausalito.

My next album, he decided, will be called *GEN plays DIN*. This is dedicated, it will say, to all old people, may they rot in hell, and especially to old, old, *old* Pearl Dedston, may she die a lingering death of a mysterious illness no drugs can cure or ease which will require an extensive post mortem by Ben while she's still alive.

There will be a picture on the album cover of legions of old people with their backs against the wall and their hands over their ears. In the picture, I'll be on the stage but instead of a flute in my hand I'll have a sub-machine gun . . . I'll be outstandingly muscular. In the other hand I'll have a dumb-bell . . .

THREE

1

'Hello, it's Carl. Are you up?'

'Yes, just about to go with Laura to the laundromat.'

'I'm so proud you hold the American record for the masters' mile. Laura told me as I was leaving.'

'Oh well, thanks. It's not that I'm so fast, only that there are hardly any women milers over forty right now. It won't be long until my record looks pretty pathetic.'

'Will you come over later?'

'Well, Jim's back from China. I think I'd better go over and see him . . .'

'Oh.'

'Call me after your practice. Laura's waiting. Goodbye, sweetheart.'

Gen and Laura walked over to the laundromat, their dirty clothes in green plastic bags. While the wash was in the machines, Laura wrote a letter to Monti in New York and Gen read the *Morning Chronicle*. With them in the laundromat were a prostitute who turned tricks by hitch-hiking along the road from Sausalito to Mill Valley, a salesman Gen knew from the running community who was always in shorts no matter what the weather or time of day to show off what was really just an adequate body, and a girl from Waldo Works, a second-hand store where Gen bought her clothes. She chatted briefly with each of them (business was good with all three), and then in walked Ben and Pearl.

Gen saw a little old lady in dress, stockings, heels, hat and gloves! She looked as if she'd been transported not only from middle America, but from middle century. Ben, in khaki pants, green pullover and plimsolls, looked as handsome as ever but, Gen thought, a little apprehensive.

She leapt to her feet. 'Welcome, Pearl. I'm Genevieve.'

115

'How do you do? I'm pleased to meet you.'

'I'm just showing Pearl around,' said Ben.

Pearl nodded graciously. 'What a nice laundromat.'

'It's new,' said Gen. 'We used to have to go all the way into town before they built this complex. But the supermarket's expensive. It's better to go to Big G. It's not too far away.'

'I don't have to watch my pennies. I'm very comfortably off.'

Gen's smile died on her lips. Pearl had given her to feel she'd purposely insulted her, accused her of penuriousness. She rallied. 'How was your trip down?'

'Satisfactory, thank you.'

All her replies seemed keenly gauged to discourage further overtures from Gen. Still, Gen tried. 'Isn't Ben's boat nice?'

'It's very nice indeed.'

Gen was relieved that it wasn't 'satisfactory'. Maybe it was good to put words into her mouth. She wished she could have a private exchange with Ben to see how everything was going, but Pearl stayed close to his side. Instead, Gen touched his shoulder, a transmittal of love and encouragement. She introduced Laura to Pearl. Laura gave Ben a kiss and Pearl a warm handshake of welcome.

As Ben and Pearl turned to leave, Gen was amazed when Pearl nodded at one of the machines, saying, 'I believe your wash is done,' as if Gen, while talking to Pearl, had been shirking her duty.

Gen found herself stepping rapidly over to the machine, like a robot.

After they had gone, Laura helped her load the dryer. She said, 'Pearl's cute. She's so tidy. Does she look anything like Ben's wife?'

'I guess so. Somewhat. But Mary was a real person, like you or me, whereas Pearl seems like the classic little old lady. I think she even puts blue in her hair. It's hard to imagine her fitting in. I hope she'll at least get some

116

comfortable shoes, not to mention a new personality. I just don't see why Ben's doing this. Maybe it seemed like a good idea when he first lost Mary and was lonely, but it must look like a horrible idea right now. It does to me.'

'Give her a chance,' Laura said. 'It's hard to come to a new place and meet new people. And imagine doing so at her age!'

'You're right, honey.' Gen wondered why Laura wouldn't give Carl a chance. She finished loading the dryer and slotted in the dimes.

'And to a place like this!' Laura added.

'What do you mean?' Gen felt offended.

'Well, it's bizarre. It isn't exactly small town USA.'

'Pearl's been living in a trailer park. That's not so different.'

'Trailer parks are conservative retirement communities for the most part. Why, Ben's the only old person around here.'

'I never think of any of us as having ages – being old, young or middle-aged.'

'Obviously not.'

Gen's heart sank. She sat there feeling middle-aged, thinking, maybe I look thirty and run a five-minute mile but it's only disguising the real facts of the case.

'Do you want me to put blue in my hair?' she asked Laura.

'No. I'm proud of you, Mom. I think you should live any way you want to – but, well, I mean, if you married Jim, it would be great. You'd be all set with a man you know well, and love, who loves you, and whom you can totally count on. Or if you stay here, living the life you always wanted, that would be good too. But this thing with Carl worries me, that's all. He'll wreck the life you've got here and not give you anything in return, except heartache. Even if you did go to live with him, what kind of life would that be?'

Gen decided to speak out. 'I don't foresee a happy life for you and Monti. It will be extremely difficult. But I'm

117

still behind you all the way.'

'But Monti's nice. And he loves me. He's a good man. *He* won't make life hard for me, society will – his or mine. We want to spend our lives together nevertheless. But Carl Knight goes from one woman to another. He just amuses himself. Maybe you'll hold his interest a little longer because you're so different. Also,' she added direly, 'I wouldn't be at all surprised if he used drugs.'

Gen's heart sank even further. Not only was she middle-aged but she was a plaything for a junkie, a temporary toy for a crazed heroin addict.

She could see their wash in the stopped dryer, a still-sodden, twisted mass, like her heart at that moment.

'This is not even to mention the thirteen years' age difference,' her daughter went on relentlessly. 'What about when he's thirty-five and you're almost fifty?'

Suddenly Gen's heart lifted. It untwisted and expanded. 'Carl says it's all up with us when he's eighty-seven. He says he refuses to go around with a hundred-year-old woman.' Gen laughed. Everything came back to its proper perspective. The love she and Carl felt for each other, their affinity, had nothing to do with age, drugs, or lifestyles. It had to do with appreciation and respect, with a rapport that was uncanny. It had to do with joy in each other. It was like her love for Laura.

She jumped up and put more dimes in the dryer. She grabbed a trolley and rolled it over. 'I remember taking your diapers to the wash,' she said. The memory seemed to descend from the blue, but was probably due to the fact that this was the first time they'd been together in a laundromat since. 'I guess every mother has paper diapers now. You'd sit in your buggy, noodling away. I'd push you and the wash all the way up the Union street hill in San Francisco, then carry you both, you and the wash, up three flights of stairs. How tired I was.' She smiled, remembering. 'But what a good baby you were. And are! Please don't worry about me. Your life is the important one round here. There's so much more of it involved in

118

any decision you make about it, whereas mine's mostly used up already. So what if Carl and I come to grief? What's a little grief at this point? Anyhow, I'm strong. I'm tough. You can't hurt steel.'

'Yeah. You looked really strong when you came home last night. Really tough.'

Gen remembered.

'I'm sorry, Mom, but I really think you should break it off with him now. Before you're in even deeper.'

Gen said nothing.

'At least,' Laura pleaded, 'don't break with Jim. Promise me that. Until you see.'

'I don't make promises any more,' Gen said.

2

'It's all over with us,' Gen said. 'I'm breaking it off.'

He looked pained. But it wasn't a look of the heart hurting, rather a look showing the difficulty he was experiencing talking to someone who'd lost her reason, someone 'touched'.

'I'm sorry. I feel like a rat. But I feel so relieved, as well, that I must be doing the right thing.'

They were at his house in the city, he in a black Eames chair, she on a beige couch in front of a panoramic view. He looked not only fatigued from his China trip, and pained from her announcement, but also mature after her weeks with Carl. He was an impressive-looking man. Maybe she *was* touched to be doing this. She felt anxious for a moment at the idea of losing him.

'You're making a big mistake, Gen,' he said, as if to stimulate her anxiety.

Again? she thought. Could I making a big mistake again? I've made so many. But imagine a life with no mistakes. How barren.

119

'I won't ask you again to marry me. This is it.'

He's threatening me with no further proposals. Well, I guess that's fair. If it's fair not to give a touched person another chance?

'I don't expect you to,' she answered. Nor would more proposals be well received, she would have liked to add. But she could never speak her thoughts aloud with Jim as she so luxuriously could with Carl.

He did a sudden about-face. Maybe he was the touched one. 'I will give you more time, Genevieve. I don't think you know what you're doing. I think you're infatuated with Carl Knight, caught in the web of his charisma. At your age you are susceptible. A last fling. I understand. I can wait it out.'

'Yes, I am caught in his web. He is very charming. But I also love him with all my heart.'

Jim sighed. He got up and made himself a scotch and soda at the little bar by the window. He dropped in the cubes of ice with tongs, then turned and looked at her thoughtfully.

I don't think I could live with a man who put ice in his drinks with tongs, she thought, bemused.

'Do you want a drink?'

'No, thanks.'

'I want you to tell Laura I'm her father.'

This abrupt change of subject made the previous discussion seem insignificant. Gen felt a twinge of fear. She'd lived with the secret so long. It was the fear of disclosure, of closed things being opened, like Pandora's box, unleashing furies and evils. 'No!' she exclaimed. 'Why?'

'She's twenty-one, a woman. She should know the truth now.'

She was only twenty, but never mind. 'It's not fair to Ted,' she said. 'We had a deal. I promised him I'd never tell.'

'So what? I thought you hated him.'

'A deal's a deal. He fulfilled his part of it. Anyhow, I don't hate him any more. That's another decision I've made, not to hate Ted.'

Am I going to hate Jim instead? she wondered, beginning to feel that she did. Now that I've finally stopped loving him? Or is it just this fright that makes me think so? Hate and fear are so closely allied, it's hard to tell one from the other. But truly I don't seem even to like him now. She scanned his face. There's something cold about him, uncaring. His face is austere and his eyes are quite reptilian, really. Carl's eyes sparkle so. When he looks at me they literally light up. I wonder why I never noticed how very lizard-like Jim is.

But have I always got to be hating someone? Maybe it's the only way I can handle hurting people. If so, it's a strange way to operate. But Jim isn't hurt, by the look of him. That is one thing he definitely isn't, I'd say.

'Jim, what would you gain by Laura's learning the truth? Then she'd know you deserted us.'

'Deserted you? Is that how you've felt all these years? That I deserted you? Or,' he said wryly, 'is that something else you've just decided?'

She smiled wanly. 'It's something else I just decided.'

'I was married at the time,' he said defensively, as if it were news to her now. 'I had two little kids, my wife was sick.'

'And stayed "sick" for twenty more years,' Gen said, 'only dying at the last because she was hit by a runaway truck.'

He looked shocked, as if she'd somehow polluted his wife's memory.

'I honestly didn't blame you at the time. Instead I blamed Ted for marrying me which, from here, seems crazy of me. I don't know why, Jim, but everything has turned all round just in these last few weeks. Maybe it's because Laura's the age I was then and it's all coming back to me. She's in love with a man who loves her as much. You think it's terrible that he's African. It would be much more terrible if he were married, didn't love her, got her pregnant, pleaded helplessness when she came to him

121

in tears, his only suggestion being that she marry someone else as soon as possible.'

'Now you do sound bitter.'

'No, it's just that I, too, am learning the truth. Maybe loving Carl has made me see differently. For the first time *ever*, I feel passionately loved.'

'The reason you see differently is because he's turning you against your friends. Against the people who have loved you for a long time. I know all about it. I've talked it over with Laura. That's why I want to give you time to come to your senses before I let you turn me down once and for all.'

'You talked to Laura before you talked to me. I think that's odd behaviour.' They're in league, she thought. My Laura, whom I would die for, has aligned herself with Jim against me.

'She called me. She's concerned.'

'I suppose she told you how she hates Carl.' Gen said this lightly to cover the pain of it.

'Yes, she did. I can't believe you'd love a man Laura hated. If someone told me so I'd say never in a million years, the two of you are so close.'

'It's a matter of principle. I can't be dictated to by her and by my love for her, any more than I would want her to be by me. A person has his own life to live. Think of parents who cast out their kids because they hate their choices. That's no kind of love. Laura must stick by me, regardless, as I would her. I was forced into my marriage with Ted – by Ted, you, my parents, and by society. I want Laura to feel free to choose whomsoever she will, with love and her own judgement the only criteria. And, since I am given another chance, I want to be free to choose too.'

Oh boy, do I sound preachy and victimized and holier-than-thou (when I'm not sounding bitter or touched). I've got to get out of here. But first, see if I can't say something kind. She didn't think she could. But why? What has he done except want to marry me?

She got to her feet and laid a hand on his arm. He was

122

still standing by the bar.

She could say, 'The great thing is that we have the most wonderful daughter in the world.'

But no. No! He only supplied the sperm. He was the donor, as they call it today. Nothing more. Ted and I raised her, loved her. Jim didn't push her and the diapers up the Union street hill and up three flights of stairs, nourish her, nurture her, instil in her the values – *such as lack of prejudice.*

She took her hand off his arm and said instead, feeling suddenly weary, 'Let me ask Ted about telling Laura.'

'You haven't talked to him for five years.'

'I know. It's time I made my peace with him.'

'Now that you're at war with me?'

'Do you feel that I am?'

'Yes.'

'Who's winning, I wonder?'

'I'll see you out.'

As she paused before the Mercedes, she saw Jim begin to look astonished, and for a second couldn't think why.

'Is this Knight's car?' he asked.

'No, this is mine. He drives a Jaguar. He says only a Jaguar can really show people how rich you are since you're always having to pay for it to be repaired. He gave me this . . . to get around in.'

'It never occurred to me you might want a car,' he said, frowning.

'It never occurred to me either,' she assured him. 'It's my first car. I must be the only American to reach forty without owning a car. Isn't it lovely? I'm getting quite fond of it.'

She got into the car and he shut the door. 'I'll call you after I've spoken to Ted. I'll let you know what he says, but we must abide by his decision. It's only fair. And, although I appreciate your wanting to give me another chance, I know Carl is the one. I will love him until I die.'

'You sound like a romantic idiot. I wish you could hear yourself.' Even as he spoke he was looking at her with new eyes, enthroned as she was in the Mercedes.

Genevieve waved and drove away, feeling like a queen (an idiot queen, but still. . .). She knew that Jim was going through a massive reassessment of their talk because of the forty-thousand-dollar vehicle.

It wouldn't have been nearly as effective an exit had I wobbled away on my bicycle.

Although it's a shame that being in this car gives me more credibility with him, imbues me with decision-making powers. Now he won't think me touched for refusing him. Now he won't think I've turned against him under the sway of Carl's mesmeric charm as Carl perniciously turns me against all my loved ones so as to love him the more.

3

'Jim Lasky is back from China and I've got to turn Genevieve against him,' Carl said. He and Rick had just been practising for three hours. Rick was exhausted, but Carl seemed stimulated. 'I've got to dishonour him in the scientific community. We'll show that he only got where he is through the work of his assistants, students mostly, who came to work with the great man. Then, his lab having made extraordinary breakthroughs in the realm of recombinant DNA technology, he appropriates information gleaned by others and leaves the university and pure research to go into private industry. He is motivated entirely by greed, and his desire for publicity and fame.' Carl paused, put a hand to his brow, and said parenthetically, 'God, he's beginning to sound exactly like me.

'Not only this,' he went on, 'but he intends to rewrite the genetic code, has in mind a horrific plan for life on this planet which would make Hitler's dreams look like baby stuff. He will create a master race, the diseaseless man. . .'

124

Rick said wearily, 'Carl, you're sick. I'm taking a hot tub.' He began to strip as he left the room.

Carl felt abandoned. His anxiety was at fever pitch about Jim Lasky's return. He feared that when Gen saw Jim again their sublimely happy weeks together would seem like mere hijinks, and she would fall into Jim's arms as she had fallen into his, giving her sweet self whole-heartedly back to Jim as she had given herself forth to him. Why had he not shown his mature side? Why had he not told her how unhappy he was until she crossed his path, how dark and bleak his heart had been until she shone her loving light therein?

The rehearsal had helped to distract him. Now he felt overwhelmed by a sense of impending doom. Abysses opened all around. He stood there by the hot tub, literally wringing his hands, feeling that wherever he stepped would be into a black bottomless hole.

Skirting the holes, picking his way along the lean crevasses, he returned to his living-room: a big room, lit by high windows, furnished with big, comfortable chairs and sofas, a thick wall-to-wall carpet for acoustic reasons as well as comfort, with bright Moroccan rugs scattered on top for beauty. A ten-foot Yamaha grand piano was piled high with sheet music, wind instruments, and two vases of flowers. A retinue of music stands huddled in its shadow.

He threw himself on to a voluptuous green velvet sofa and dialled Gen's number with his wireless phone.

No answer. Wait, someone was picking up the phone at last. Thank God! (Thank you, God. I'll pay you hand-somely for this. You do like money, don't you? How I wish that you did.)

'Hello?' It was Laura.

'Hello, this is Carl. Is your mother there?'

'She's gone to the city to see Jim.'

'When did she go?'

'Hours ago.'

'Hours? And she's not back yet?'

'That's right.'

'Did she say when she'd be back?'

'No.'

'Tell her I called, then. Thanks. Thank you ever so.'

Carl put the telephone aside.

How cold Laura sounded. How could she be so cold and unfeeling, so *mean*? Why? Why was she? Her voice had entered his ear in an icy trickle that was now filling his entire insides. He felt so frozen he could hardly walk. He staggered to the piano stool, sat down.

I should compose something. It would make me feel better. It always does. Foolproof.

But his mind was frozen too, and his fingers. He felt like a zombie, a diseaseless zombie.

He got up and, in an exaggerated zombie walk, arms held stiffly in front of him, he went to his bedroom, another huge cheerful room, dedicated to good light, good sound, and comfort. Here he lit a candle. Soon he was melting some heroin crystals in a spoon over the candle flame, then filling a syringe with the resultant solution. He released it into the vein on his inner forearm.

The rush came and with it life, warmth, feeling and music. A magnificent orchestra was playing a short contrapuntal piece, an invention, which was the heavenly sound of abysses closing . . . heralding the sublime soundlessness of oblivion.

4

Gen decided to go and see her ex-husband and get it over with. He lived on the other side of the city, on Telegraph Hill. Jim was on Twin Peaks and Carl was in between, on Pacific Heights. All three men delighted in being on top. Only she bided at sea level. What did this mean, if anything? She would think about it later.

She contemplated stopping at Carl's house to see him, but hesitated to disturb him during rehearsal. GEN was getting ready for a Japanese tour. Besides, this was her day for clearing the decks towards her new life with Carl. Tomorrow could be for Carl alone.

Driving the steep streets, she had an uneasy feeling that she had made a deal with Jim, a diabolical pact. He would release her from her engagement if she told Laura he was her father. It was like a pay-off — with him getting what he most wanted, without having to include her in the package after all.

It was as if she were somehow bartering in her daughter's provenance.

Gen thought she had better stop at a phone box and telephone Ted. It would hardly be fair to appear un-expectedly at his door after five years.

As it was Saturday morning, he'd have slept until twelve and be having breakfast with the paper in front of some sports event on TV. Though he might have changed his habits. She certainly had.

He sounded cordial at the other end of the line and invited her to come on ahead.

In front of his apartment house, she felt nervous and unhappy.

Why am I doing this? I don't want to see him. I want to keep on comfortably hating him. My aversion to Ted is so old, it's like a pet one can't possibly put to sleep even though it's begun to smell and to pee indoors.

As she was convincing herself that she could have this interview at some other time (although she couldn't think just when) a man came out of the front door. He started to pass her and stopped. 'Say, are you Genevieve?'

'Yes, I am.'

He was a New Wave-looking young man: curly hair, short on top, longer about the neck, an earring, tight jeans, a zebra-striped T-shirt, black jacket.

'I'm Ted's friend. I've always wanted to meet you, but he wanted me out before you arrived.' He held out his hand, smiling, and Gen shook it. 'My name is Sebastian Smith.'

'What a beautiful name. I always wanted a son called Sebastian.'

'Really?' It seemed to please him inordinately. He beamed upon her. 'You and Ted haven't seen each other for such a long time, I imagine you're nervous. I know he is. Oh, he'd hate me to say that' – Sebastian laughed a little breathlessly – 'but it's true. And entirely under-standable. I'll tell you one thing: he's always spoken of you in the kindest terms. I think it's been a grief to him that your split was so decisive. But sometimes that's the only way, don't you think? Build anew, as it were. I understand. And, in the long run, I think it was best for him, too. My, I am meddling, aren't I? It would be better if he said these things to you himself. It's just that' – he paused, pondering – 'I don't think he will. And I care.'

'I can tell that you do.' Genevieve felt tears prick her eyes. How absurd. It was only that she was feeling so emotional in general. 'Well,' she said, 'I'd better go in. Thank you,' she said vaguely, but meaning it. He had helped. 'Thank you, Sebastian.'

He shook her hand again. 'Ciao, Genevieve.'

She mounted the steps and rang the third-floor apart-ment bell. Ted buzzed her in and was standing on the landing with the door open when she reached the top.

'Hello, Ted.' She ducked her head and went past him.

As of yore, the apartment was furnished in fierce good taste, but there were some bits of colour and warmth: an afghan thrown over the back of the sofa, plants beyond the mandatory Shefflera and Benjamina, which delicately flowered and required real care. As well there were tissue paper collages, combining the same subtle, almost fra-grant delicacy of the flowers.

The view was of the Bay to the east. In the wide sky, stradivarius clouds imitated the sweep of water. (No, no, Stradivarius was a violin-maker, not a cloud formation.)

Ted, when she forced herself to glance at him, looked in

128

good form. They both seemed to have shed pounds, years, and cares when they shed each other. He wore khaki trousers and a white shirt.

'May I offer you anything to drink? Coffee?'

'No, thanks, Ted.'

'You look wonderful.'

'Thank you. So do you. I like your apartment.'

'Let me show you Laura's room. She has her own room, even though she's here so rarely. I think it's good for her to know she has a home for ever, regardless. This is no reflection on your houseboat,' he added hastily.

He did seem a little nervous, but cheerful. She'd forgotten what an essentially good-natured person he was. It suited her imagination to portray him as a bogeyman.

He showed her a charming room, white, of course, but softened by peach-coloured drapes and a lovely old quilt of varying shades of yellow and white. Of course, even the most fervent contemporary designers appreciated folk-art now. Quilts and afghans were *de rigueur*. Nevertheless, it was a lovely room for Laura: spacious, feminine, and cosy. As Gen glanced at some of the titles on the bookshelf, he explained, 'Laura sent those on from college when she went to England, so I put them there for her.'

Laura has this whole other life, Gen thought wonderingly. Her daughter had wisely resolved never to talk to either parent about the other and they had learned not to inquire. Whenever Laura left her to stay with Ted, it was as if she was going to another country – even when Gen too was living in San Francisco. She felt rather like a spy in enemy territory, except that Ted was showing it to her with such pride and pleasure. Gen felt glad of this 'home for Laura', because her houseboat did not provide one, and if she moved in with Carl, she thought sadly, Laura would not want to come there. It was good she had this lovely room 'regardless' and 'for ever'. It warmed her to Ted. All her apprehension fell away. But it made the purpose of her visit harder, seeing how very much Laura meant to him.

'Ted,' she began, when they were back in the living-room. 'Laura's real father has come back into my life and he wants to tell her the truth.'

'I am her real father.'

'Well, her blood father . . . wants to say so.

'No. I am Laura's father. That was the agreement.'

He was adamant.

'She is almost twenty-one,' Gen tried. (Why?) 'It won't change her love for you or her relationship with you. It seems right that she should know.'

He walked agitatedly about the room, picking things up and smashing them down. 'It isn't right. He has no claim. It was our agreement. How dare he come forward now?'

'I know,' she said weakly.

'Does she know this man?'

'Yes.'

'It will make her feel she owes allegiance to him. More of her time will have to be shared and even less will come to me. Or . . . are you planning to marry him? Is that why?'

'I was . . .

'You've never told me who he is. I don't want to know. Thank God you can keep a secret so well. And I want you still to keep mine. Ours. Laura is *my* daughter. *My* family. She's my only family. I will never marry again.'

Should she say she had met Sebastian? Yes. 'I met your friend as I was coming in. It's made me understand a lot . . . about us, about me, my feelings . . . it's such a shame, really, that we weren't of Laura's generation. Everything is easier for them, more open. So much is more available.'

'Abortions for one thing. You might have lost Laura.'

'Yes.'

They paused to imagine the unimaginable, a world with no Laura.

'I'm glad you met Sebastian,' Ted decided. 'I didn't want you to but I'm glad you did, if it helps you.' He relaxed a little, and sat down. She sat too. He lit a cigarette, drew deeply.

130

Genevieve was remembering their sex together. It was never good. She had blamed herself, feeling it was because of her lack of love and passion. She understood now how very much it had been against Ted's nature, something he performed as a duty. She had done her duty in return, never dreaming that for him it was probably not only without pleasure but a revolt to his whole system and psyche. He would often fall asleep on the sofa and in the early years, concerned for his comfort, she would come and wake him, bring him to bed. Later, she prayed he would not come to bed and want sex, or that if he did it would be over quickly. It always was over quickly and their joinings became more and more infrequent.

She thought she was frigid, dysfunctional, and felt she was failing twofold.

The day came when she could not embrace him at all, no matter how fleetingly. Then it became impossible to remain his wife.

Ted also appeared to be thinking back.

'Did you have lovers during the time we were married?' she asked painfully.

'No! No! I honestly didn't know. It was only after you left me that I . . . began to give myself a chance . . . at happiness.'

'Do you think if you'd married a woman who loved you it would have been different?'

'No. And anyhow, I loved you. You were the only woman I ever wanted to be with. We'd been such good friends through our childhood. I felt comfortable with you. And I loved Laura from the start. I wanted to be the father of your child. I still do. But now it hasn't to do with you but with her. I'm sorry, Genevieve. I'm glad to be able to tell you at last that I'm sorry for all the years it was so awful for you.'

'I'm sorry, too. I guess it was wasted years for both of us. But we did have Laura, who was such a joy to us both.' It was easy to talk to him now. The words flew out. 'I began to hate you, Ted, because I couldn't love you. I

131

hated becoming so cold, shrivelling up.'

'It was my fault. Only I just didn't know. We were both so repressed, really, so unable to communicate in any helpful way.'

'I'm glad you found out, Ted. It must have been hard. It was hard for me, too, to begin to take lovers, to begin to feel. And, actually, well, you see' – she blushed – 'I'm in love again now. For the first time in twenty years! I guess that's what finally allowed me to come to you, freed me to come and say these things. Laura's father's plea was just a pretext, but a true one.'

Ted grew agitated again. The blood rushed to his face, then drained. 'If he tells her, I'll kill him.'

'Surely not,' Gen gasped.

'Yes, it means that much to me. In fact, it means even more now. Lovers come and go but family doesn't. I want . . . I want to have grandchildren. If Laura knew I wasn't her father, it would change everything. Everything!'

Driving home, Genevieve realized she hadn't asked Ted if Laura knew he was gay. But after his murder threat, one could hardly go blithely on with other subjects. That had pretty well concluded their talk. What a talk! She felt wrung out.

There were shoes and shorts in the boot. Why not park at Fort Mason and run to the bridge and back? Seven good fast miles with the scent of the sea in her nostrils and the fog in her hair.

Or . . . Again she thought longingly of Carl, whose rehearsal would be over by now.

But no. She had to absorb her talk with Ted first. A run would stimulate her as well.

That was the genius of running. While your body was moving merrily along, your brain was achieving these miracles of absorption, perspective, and sense. It was masterfully shuffling and filing information from lobe to lobe, cell to cell, until everything was in its place and you felt giddy with the perfect balance and order of your psyche – or with the marvellous illusion of balance and order.

But where, into what lobe, what cell, would the murder threat go? How far would she have to run to absorb that one? Or gain the illusion of absorbing it?

It couldn't be a new idea to Ted. He must always have wanted to murder Jim and now that he was in touch with his feelings he could say so. And now, because of Jim's threat to tell Laura, Ted had a handle for his bloodlust. No, wrong. It *was* a new feeling for Ted. It was probably she who had always wanted to murder Jim, not he. He only wanted to now. He had spoken in heat. He was upset. He would cool down. Anyhow, Ted didn't even know Jim's name, nor that he lived in San Francisco. She was not going to get in a fit of apprehension. But she was still going to have that run.

From the boot she pulled out yellow shorts and a pink shirt, good colours for fog.

Ted, smoking not running, was also absorbing their talk. Later, it would seem obvious to him that if two people had lived together for fifteen years without communicating, then, after five years of unbroken silence, the chance of reaching a perfect understanding when the silence is at last breached is nil. No matter what their personal growth in the meantime, the chances are nil.

This did not occur to Ted until later.

Presently, looking back over their talk, Ted did not allow for their inability to communicate and misinterpreted the whole thing.

He concluded that Gen had come to him because she was once again in love with Laura's blood father. It was because they were to be married that the villain wanted Laura to know he was her real father. Understandably, Gen too might want it in the open at last. Although she might try to dissuade the man from any revelation, she

133

would not pass on Ted's threat, which had only made her gasp. Therefore Ted must threaten the man himself, dissuade him once and for all. It would be a simple matter to find out his identity.

He sighed and put out his cigarette. In a way it had been nice keeping his life wholly separate from Gen. Sebastian was a world-class meddler. He shouldn't have told him Gen was coming. He should have got rid of him on some other pretext. But he'd learned that loving a person didn't give you control over them. Especially Sebastian.

5

When Gen got back to *Loiter Longer*, Ben, Pearl and Sally were there with Laura. Pearl had been with Ben five days now. She was a nutritionist who had spent her spinsterhood ('no one says spinster any more') living at different girls' boarding schools and later at some private men's clubs, planning menus. Gen thought that after five days she must have heard the last word that possibly could be said about nutrition, but apparently not. Pearl was still instructing them, and clearly there was an infinitude of information on Pearl's tongue about fats alone, not even broaching the vast territory of vitamins and calories. Astonishingly, both Sally and Laura hung on every word. Sally, like many runners, was always in the grip of some many-tentacled diet, but why Laura? Ben, of course, being such a gentleman, gave Pearl his full and undivided attention . . . but poor Ben! Genevieve's heart went out to him. What if Pearl stayed? What if he couldn't get rid of her? She seemed quite settled. She apparently perceived their houseboat community as another in her life's long line of boarding schools.

Gen hadn't had a chance to have a private talk with Ben

during Pearl's stay, so wrapped up had she been in her own life and he with his visitor, but she mustn't forsake him. She must let him know she would stand by him through thick and thin. They could plot together to get rid of Pearl. Somehow she must contrive to let Ben know that she was available for even the most ignoble action.

Felicitously, as they were leaving, Pearl turned back for one last word to Sally about cholesterol. Gen seized her chance.

'Ben,' she whispered, 'about Pearl . . .'

Ben smiled and shook his head back and forth like one stunned. 'Isn't she wonderful!' he said.

Sally and Laura had moved on to the subject of veterinary science and Sally was telling Laura about an injured Arab mare she'd spent the morning with. Her luminous light blonde head bent towards Laura's sleek dark blonde one. Two beautiful women, Gen thought, strong women: Laura daring to love a man from another land, a dark, troubled land; Sally daring to take her body to the limit of its potential so as to dream of going further.

Although so much younger than herself, they both had an inner calm and steadiness of purpose that she did not possess. And they were good women. From here they seemed almost holy, but perhaps that was because they were such a feast to the eyes after Pearl, whose tiny philosophy was forged from a life of inconsequence in which she dared neither to love nor bear children, do deeds or dream dreams. Instead she planned meals. Not for her the adventure of womanhood. Why strive for your fullest potential if you can become smaller, narrower, more petty, pinched, and purposeless.

'You're thinking mean thoughts about Pearl,' said Laura, smiling. 'I can tell. You know why, don't you? You're jealous because Ben is so nuts about her.'

'I honestly didn't know he was until just now.' Gen pondered this surprising and interesting accusation.

135

'And just now is when you started thinking mean thoughts.'

'No, I've thought them all along.'

'It's natural,' said Sally. 'I'm jealous of your loving Carl because he takes you away from me.'

'But I don't love you any the less,' Gen protested.

'I know. But sexual relationships always take precedence over friendships. They have to. They take so much energy.'

'I wonder why they do? I wonder why we can't love our lovers in the same easy-going way we love our friends – without jealousy, dependence, possessiveness – in short, without scenes.'

'Territoriality,' said Sally. 'The ape that is still in us.'

'Thus spake the animal doctor. But I don't believe we come from apes.'

Sally looked astonished and dismayed.

'It's true,' Laura said. 'My mother's the only educated person I know who doesn't think so. And she's one of the few who's actually read Darwin, too.'

'Darwin,' Gen scoffed. 'That old seasick humbug.'

'Well, where did man begin, then?' asked Sally.

'The garden of Eden. And that's where all the troubles between the sexes began too. But I don't blame God or Adam or Eve or the serpent, I blame the fruit. Philosophically, I'm a fruitist. Shall I elaborate?'

'No!' both of them exclaimed. 'Please don't.'

'You could call your love story with Carl the flautist and the fruitist,' said Sally.

They all laughed.

'Before I forget, Mom, Carl called around noon.'

Sally got up. 'I'm going to leave my bike here and run home, if that's all right.'

'Fine.'

'Do you want to run part way?'

'I've already run in the city. Let's run together tomorrow.'

They hugged each other and parted.

Gen poured wine for herself and Laura. 'Sit tight. I'm going to tell you something that will astound you. I've just come from a visit to your father. A nice visit.' She smiled.

'Oh, Mom, that's wonderful.' Laura gave her a hug. 'Imagine! After all these years!'

'Yes, we've made our peace with each other at last. He looks very well and we had a good talk.'

'Did you meet Sebastian?' Laura asked tentatively.

'I'm glad you asked. I was wondering how to mention the subject without giving it away if you didn't know.'

'Dad used to make him leave when I came to visit, but I would still sometimes see him. Sebastian made sure that I did. Then, when I realized what was happening, I told Dad to let Sebastian stay. After all, it's like a marriage. It didn't seem right to drive him off, to pretend.'

'Did it disturb you when you realized?'

'Well, by then I'd had friends who were gay and I understood a lot about it. One thing I can say for you and Daddy is that you brought me up entirely without pre-judice. You can't imagine how rare that is.'

All Gen could think now was how unjust Laura was to embrace Sebastian and not Carl. 'Yes,' she answered. 'I know it's rare, and I'm glad we succeeded. But . . .' She paused, and said with extreme difficulty, 'But now it seems you're just tolerant towards those who most need it. You're all heart towards the old, the gay, the black – but Carl, who's white, young, and brilliant, you won't give an inch to. You won't open your heart one tiny bit even though it means everything in the world to me.'

Gen began to cry. She fell apart. This was what she meant by lacking inner tranquillity. But the whole day had been a terrible strain. She couldn't help it. And the wine, too. The wine had gone straight to her head as if it had made a bet with the bottle before being poured. She took another gulp, wondering if it could be an antidote for itself.

Laura, seeing her mother cry, an unfamiliar sight, began to weep too. 'I'm sorry, Mom.'

137

'Boohoo,' wept Gen. She was one of the few people in the world who actually said boohoo when she cried. This interested Laura so much that she stopped crying herself, perhaps feeling she could not contend with such a superior sound.

'You've just been so mean about him right from the start,' Gen persisted. 'What if I'd been that way with Monti? How would you feel? You'd be so torn, so wretched. I've tried not to let your feelings influence me, not to let it get me down, but it does. I can't stand it. It breaks my heart.'

'I'll try. I'll try to like him. I'm sorry!'

'I'm sorry for getting so upset. It's been a long day. It wasn't easy going to see your father. And Jim. I saw Jim, too. That wasn't easy either, let me tell you.'

'Did you . . .? I hope you didn't . . .'

'Yes, I did,' Gen said defensively. Her tears were spent. She got up and blew her nose. 'Of course I did.' She went to the kitchen sink and splashed cold water on her face, wiping it with a paper towel. 'I broke off our engagement. It was the only decent thing to do. It would be most unfair to string him along. We'll still be close friends,' she said dubiously. 'It didn't seem to bother him much. I don't think he loves me, Laura, now that I begin to see what love is. He just wanted to marry me, have me.' Us, she amended to herself. Just Laura, she thought as a codicil to the amendment.

Laura began putting salad together for dinner while Gen grilled some red snapper fillets and set the table. These are pleasing, soothing activities, she thought. Maybe there's something to Pearl's life after all.

After dinner, Laura said, 'Don't forget to call Carl.'

'Oh, right! Thanks, sweetheart, for reminding me.' She gave her a kiss. Laura's reminder showed that she was going to try to like him and the idea of her mother with him. It was a breakthrough.

She dialled his number but there was no answer, not even from his machine.

138

6

Carl was on a heroin binge. It lasted for three days. He showed up for rehearsals each morning, then disappeared. Rick kept an eye on him. He wasn't too worried. He thought it would only last as long as Carl's cache and that would be it. It was a token binge, a last salute to his old life before settling down with Genevieve. Rick thought it was Carl's insecurity that had caused it. He knew Carl couldn't understand why Gen wouldn't throw up her existing life and let herself become enveloped in his, as if she were a young girl whose only ambition was to leave home and marry. At the same time, Rick knew it was partly because she was so independent, satisfied with her life, desired by other men, that Carl was drawn to her. The other part was the famous 'affinity' he kept talking about.

It was still pretty soon after the coma. He had hoped that episode had scared him away from the stuff for ever. But he sensed that Carl was being careful. His actions were not as self-destructive as they appeared.

The life they led was in truth a terrible life. Rick could handle it. Carl could not.

On the fourth day, pale and ten pounds lighter, walking like an old man and even, Gen noticed, a little grey around the temples, Carl explained Rick's thinking to her. They were alone on *Loiter Longer*, Laura having gone to her father's.

Carl had arrived with an enormous bouquet of orange tigerlilies mixed with some small white flower and Gen was arranging them as he talked.

He lay on the sofa, subsiding into the peace of lapping water and Gen's warm and gentle atmosphere.

'Rick thinks I did it because of you. He's probably told

139

you all this. He's probably been giving you all sorts of bloody attention in the guise of looking after you for me but really wooing you on his own. It's classic best-friend behaviour. Tell me honestly – have you slept with Rick during the last three days?'

'I haven't even seen Rick, you idiot. I didn't know you'd been on this stupid binge until just now. Rick told me you were composing a jazz suite and couldn't be disturbed.' Gen started to cry.

'Why are you crying?'

'I don't know.' She gulped. 'I've been on a crying binge. I can have binges, too, you know. You're not the only one. Everything seems to make me cry. It's probably the menopause. I didn't get my period. But this time I'm crying over you. I hate the fact that you take heroin, that you risk your life in that stupid way when you know how dangerous it is.'

'Nonsense. I've used it on and off for years and only almost died once. I'm not an addict. I don't have an addictive personality. You're the addict, with your running every goddamn day.'

'Just to look at you breaks my heart. You look like an old man. Why did you do it?'

'That's what I'm trying to tell you, if you'll listen. Rick says it's because you won't come and live with me, because you won't say you love me more than anyone else on earth and give up all your friends and family and houseboat and fiancé and come and live with me and be my love at once. He says it's my monstrous ego that expects you to do this and that I should be patient and let you come when you're ready.'

'I'm getting ready, I really am.'

'Wait a minute. That's what Rick says. Now hear what I say. I took heroin because I'm bored. I'm bored with you and our love affair and Laura's attitude and Ben and Pearl. I'm bored to death with Pearl. If I have to listen to her talking about food once more I'm going to show her what partially digested food looks like by puking all over

140

her recipe books.'

Gen smiled.

'Don't laugh. I'm bored with your running and having to hear about it but never actually seeing you run because you do it with your boring running friends or alone. I'm bored with Sally and her rosy cheeks. Then, when I try to bring someone interesting into our lives, like that little girl from the ship's chandler, you create the most hideous scene, just walk away without even saying goodbye.'

'I did say goodbye. At least, I said, "I'm going now." And anyhow, a lover isn't supposed to be someone to amuse your idle hours. If you want to be entertained, hire a court jester.'

'That's not a bad idea.'

'I'll be your court jester if it'll help you stay clean . . .'

Carl rolled his eyes. 'No one says clean any more. . .'

'I don't care what dopers say!' she flashed at him. 'Who cares what the chic word is to describe the use of poison? All I'm saying is that I'll do anything, be anything, if it will help you not to use the stuff. I mean it, Carl.' She opened her arms. 'Come, give me a hug and kiss.'

'No.'

'Please, my dearest love. I've missed you so much. I do love you. I've broken my engagement with Jim. I told him I was in love with you. Then I even went to see my ex-husband and made my peace with him. I told him I was in love. So, you see, I'm getting ready to live happily ever after . . . and probably I will come to live with you, if only to get away from Pearl.' She laughed. 'But not yet,' she added. 'Not quite yet, but soon. There's one last thing I have to resolve before I can give you all my attention.'

Carl gave her the kiss she so ardently desired. She took off his clothes and her own and made passionate love to which Carl submitted with a lordly air. Once aroused he could not maintain this simulated insouciance, however, nor did he want to. He was too hungry for her and for her hunger. He wanted to feel and taste and know her need for him, feel her thrill to his entry, run with her to the finish,

141

staying with her breath for breath until they could burst together through the barrier of their bodies and minds to their souls.

(Yes, souls, God. Her sweet white one and my briny black one touched each other just now and mine was made anew.)

'Do you know you're the best lover in the whole world? I suppose you do know. I suppose every woman has told you. Or it could be that I love you so much you just seem incomparable. You're so exciting. You only have to look at me sideways and I begin to feel wild with desire for you. I tremble from head to toe. Did I ever tell you about Winchester? I was sitting by the river Avon, writing you that card about the diver . . .'

'William Walker.'

'Yes. And I thought about you and our kiss in Laura's bedsit, and I moaned aloud. I was so embarrassed, because there was a fisherman nearby. I thought he heard me moan for you.'

'The angler,' he said. 'We call them anglers.'

'Yes, and what was it William Walker said to the King?'

'I'm proud to be able to help in so grand a work.'

'Did you know about him before my card?'

'No,' he lied.

'That's good. I wanted to tell you something you might not know and share it with you.'

'Let's get back to what a lover I am.'

'All right. Well, you just seem to love everything about it. And you stay yourself. Some men seem to vacate their bodies when they make love, as if they're embarrassed to be there. Or else there's an underlying hostility in their caresses, or they're pretending the whole time, imagining some conception they have of themselves as a lover, some style they've decided on . . .'

'How many lovers have you had? It sounds like legions.'

'Only five.' She still did not count Jim. Nor, apparently, had she ever counted Ted, poor Ted, or yet included Carl in the count. In truth, she simply wasn't a counter. 'I

142

guess that really doesn't make me such an authority. How about you?'

'Four.'

'What a liar you are.' She laughed. 'Four. I bet! Although it could be true. Once you've set up the precedent for lying a lot you're able to tell the truth disguised as a lie. I'm on to your tricks. The important thing is, am I your last lover?'

'So far, you're my last. You're the first I've asked to live with me. And to die with me. Will you die with me?'

'Yes,' she said solemnly. 'I'll stay with you until one of us dies.'

'Will you throw your body on my pyre?'

'We don't have funeral pyres in America.'

'Well, pie, then.'

'Yes, I'll throw myself on your funeral pie.'

They collapsed with laughter.

Some colour had come back to Carl's cheeks and some brightness to his eyes. His temples stayed grey.

7

They decided to have supper on *Loiter Longer* and then go to a movie. While Gen sautéed some mushrooms and green onions for an omelette, Carl walked out to get some wine at the supermarket next to the laundromat. It was dusk. A huge orange moon was rising in the east, looking as if, Carl thought, against all the rules of the Universe Committee, it had been popping planetary steroids.

It was while contemplating its extraordinary size, and thinking what a spider's web it made of the Oakland Bay bridge, that Carl felt a large muscular arm encircle his neck in a vice-like grip. A voice whispered in his ear.

'Don't tell Laura. This is just to let you know how serious I am. If you tell Laura, I'm going to kill you.'

143

He applied enough pressure to assure Carl he knew how to kill, by strangulation anyhow, then released him, at the same time giving a forward push so that Carl fell to his hands and knees.

He twisted round to get a look at the man who, although striding purposefully away, was not exactly fleeing the scene. He was tall, large-armed, fair, not young.

'I won't,' Carl promised, shouting after the man. But his voice came out in a thin, uncarrying croak. 'I won't tell Laura. No sir.'

He got shakily to his feet and walked slowly on to the supermarket, massaging his neck. Don't tell Laura what? he wondered. How do I even know what not to tell her? Kill me? Did he say he'd kill me and that he was serious? The man's mad. If I don't know what I'm not supposed to tell her, I could easily tell her by mistake and get mistakenly killed. This is probably some vile plot of Gen's to keep our love affair from being boring and keep me off heroin thereby. I should tell her it's not *that* boring.

Don't tell Laura what? I'm not going to tell Laura anything from now on, if I'm even going to speak to her at all. It's going to be strictly greetings and partings: hello, how are you, goodbye, see you later, nice day – words that could not possibly be deemed even to hint at revelation.

God! Carl took a deep breath to see if his oesophagus was working. Doesn't he know I'm a flute player? Has he no respect? Couldn't he have threatened me with a gun to my head like a decent murderer?

'A bottle of Dom Perignon, please,' he whispered to the wine merchant. 'No? Well, do you have Mumms, then? That's more fitting, actually, since mum's the word from now on as far as telling Laura is concerned.'

Once back, as soon as he told Gen, who was all wide-eyed open-mouthed attention, he could tell that she understood, that she knew who the man was, and what it was that Laura was not to be told. In short, it was obvious to the meanest eye that she instantly grasped the entire picture. But did she hasten to put him in it?

While he appreciated her sympathy and the concern she lavishly bestowed, he was much more interested in getting to the bottom of the thing. After all, it was his life they were talking about.

Gen wasn't a good liar but she was a world-class evader and temporizer. Even when he put a direct question to her she could spin rings of words around him until he was quite dazzled by her ability to confuse. He loved her for these verbal pyrotechnics.

In time, he realized that he could not extract the truth from her if he continued to whisper. Whispers did not carry the authority of the solidly-voiced word, and anyhow he was only doing it to milk the last drop of sympathy. So, after a show of massage, champagne-gargle, deep breathing and throat clearing, he said in his normal voice plus added emphasis, 'I want to know who attacked me and what not to tell Laura. I want to know this now.'

'Well, all I can think,' said Gen rather miserably, 'is that it was Ted Randall, my ex-husband. Your description of a tall man with big arms could fit him. Was he blond?'

'Yes.'

'It must have been Ted. There's no one else it could be to have it make sense. I believe he mistook you for Jim Lasky. That's all I can think. Ted has never met Jim. He probably assumed you were Jim because he saw you come from my houseboat, and because of your heroin binge.'

'What does my binge have to do with it?' Carl expostulated, amazed at this new move.

'I hate the way you say "my binge" as if it were something you were fond of, like a pet. You sound so protective.'

'Answer the question,' he said sternly.

'Because it's made you look so old. Jim is fifty! You're only twenty-nine and Ted mistook you for Jim. Normally he never would have.'

'If he doesn't know Jim, how could he know how old he was?' Carl asked keenly.

145

'Well,' she evaded, 'he just knows.'

'OK. I accept that it was Ted mistaking me for Jim. What is Jim not to tell Laura?'

He waited with bated breath. Now they were at the heart of the matter. This was it.

'I'm sorry. I can't tell you that.'

'What? Did you say you won't tell me? Are you kidding? This is me, Carl, your nearest and dearest, the same man for whom you said only moments ago you'd do anything, *be* anything. . .'

Gen's eyes looked distressed but otherwise her face was grim and stony. Her lips were sealed. Carl begged, he abased himself, he threatened, he left her for ever, came back a minute later. He wept. Yes, he actually wept. Real tears. And meant them, too. He was unbelievably hurt that she would keep a secret from him, the lover she had moaned for by the river Avon – especialy such an important secret as this obviously was.

He went through his whole bag of tricks. In the end he offered her money. She could name the price.

'I'm not going to tell you, Carl.'

He was full of admiration. In his whole life he'd never known a woman who could keep a secret, especially from him.

This took over an hour, through dinner and coffee. He was exhausted. 'OK. I give up. Just remember this. If Jim tells Laura this thing that can't be told, who gets killed? Me. Is that just?'

'No, it's unjust and it's scary, too. I'll tell Jim not to tell her. I meant to do it today, and yesterday, too. I was putting off the unpleasantness. It didn't seem such a desperate matter then, of course.'

'Was Ted ever violent when you were married to him?'

'No, not at all. This obviously means a great deal to him. Do you think we all have violence in us when something matters enough? It's frightening to think so. When he said he would kill Jim if he told Laura, I didn't worry about it too much because I knew he didn't know who Jim

146

was. When I told him I was in love, he must have assumed it was with Jim. Probably Laura had mentioned I was engaged to a fifty-year-old man so, when he saw this *old, old* man tottering out of my door, he said to himself, that has to be Jim Lasky. If he'd seen you with Pearl he would have thought you were Ben, but being with me made you look younger than eighty and nearer to fifty.'

'That's very funny. I thought lovers weren't supposed to be a source of idle amusement. One can hire a court jester for that, you said.'

'Right. Sorry.'

'I'd like you to call Jim Lasky now. I want him to know at once about this misdirected threat.'

'Very well. But I won't mention the threat. It will be enough to tell him not to tell Laura. Please forgive me if I ask you not to listen to the conversation.'

'I won't listen.' He sat down and covered his ears.

'You'll have to go outside while I call. I'm sorry.'

'What? I can't hear you.'

'You can too.'

Carl went outside, tramped loudly up the plank. Then tiptoed down and put his keen ears (perfect pitch) to the partly-open kitchen window.

'Jim, this is Genevieve. I hope I'm not disturbing you. That's good. Well, the reason I'm calling . . .'

Carl heard murmurs, then nothing. He looked through the window and saw that she had carried the phone into the bedroom and shut the door. Blast! There was no bedroom window, only the sliding deck door and he would have to swim to reach the deck. Should he? No, it wasn't worth it. There was no assurance that he would learn the secret from her side of the conversation, it would be ignominious to get wet in the process of learning nothing, and anyhow he didn't know how to swim.

'Carl!' Gen was calling from the front door.

'Here I am. How did it go?'

'He's rather upset. He wouldn't promise me. But he said he'd meet me tomorrow for lunch and talk about it.

147

He'll do nothing until then, at least.'

'Oh, good, then I have until tomorrow lunchtime to live.'

Gen cast her eyes down wretchedly.

Carl gave her his most winsome look, which wasn't easy as at this point he was feeling pretty damned pissed. 'Genevieve,' said he. 'I am hurt, I am deeply offended, that you will not share this secret with me, that you are actually closing me out of an obviously intimate part of your life, making two men appear to mean more to you than I do. How would you feel? How would you react in the same circumstances?'

'I am trying to respect the feelings and wishes of both those men. It is very difficult for me and you are not helping by making me feel bad about it. You are not being a guerdon.'

'A what?' he asked sharply.

One of her tricks was to pull unknown words on him when they were arguing, to throw him off the track, and it always worked.

'I mean that you are not fortifying me in my time of trouble. As my lover and helpmeet you should strengthen and encourage, be my comfort and reward. That's what a guerdon is, a reward.'

'I'll be damned if I'll be your fucking guerdon. Your ex-husband comes and strangles me and you ask me to be your reward. I'm going!' He paused at the door and said ominously, 'I'm taking this into my own hands. Good night. And please notice that I am walking, not "tottering", to the door, you bitch.'

'But, Carl, sweetheart. . . '

The door shut behind him. A second later it opened, and Carl put his head through and said to Gen, who was looking rather dejected, 'I love you. I think you are magnificent to keep this secret so well, but . . .'

She threw herself into his arms. 'I love you with all my heart. Thank you for understanding about the secret.'

It was fine of her. She made him feel noble for being

148

understanding when he'd acted like an idiot the entire
evening, been rude and snivelling. He knew that deep
down she must be happy to see him go at last, but she was
still able to be gracious and loving. Nevertheless he
addressed her gravely. 'I must tell you that I do not
believe in secrets. They are dangerous. When you bury a
truth it becomes foul and slimy. This secret must be
unearthed and given light and air. It must be told to
everyone concerned, especially me.'

Gen began to wring her hands and look unhappy again.
'Promise me you won't take it into your own hands,
though, Carl. Please leave it to me. Please.'

'I won't. . .'

'Take it into your own hands?'

'I won't promise to leave it to you. Good night.'

8

Carl meant what he said about secrets. He loathed and
feared them. His parents had secrets when he was a boy
and he always felt these had to do with their lack of love for
each other and him, all in all making his childhood absolute hell. He believed in openness among friends, family,
and lovers. Lies were all right, but not secrets. Lies were
harmless and amusing and often helped things along.
Secrets were troublemakers. And this one of Gen's was big
trouble.

The next morning he woke up still thinking about it.
Mentally he listed his thoughts: Ted Randall does not
want his daughter, Laura, told something. Jim Lasky
wants to tell it. Gen, apparently, could go either way, tell
or not tell. Jim Lasky would gain from it. Ted Randall
would lose.

Ted is willing to murder to keep it from being disclosed
to Laura. Therefore, if the man's not mad, it's some secret!

What do I want out of all this?

I want Gen to love me and come to live with me and I want to know what Laura shouldn't be told.

What don't I want?

I don't want to murdered by mistake.

Should I pass on the threat to Jim Lasky, pretending to be Ted?

No, I'd never pull it off. I'm not big and strong enough. I haven't used the Nautalis machine once. Nor am I intimidating. I'm just a humble flute player, a flabby minstrel. Also, Jim Lasky may know me by sight. I'm damned famous, after all. And if I passed on the threat by telephone, my English accent would be a dead give-away.

Should I seek out this Ted Randall and tell him of his mistake?

Why not? Excellent idea.

It was only seven thirty a.m. when Carl was buzzed into Ted Randall's apartment house. A rumpled young homosexual, still in pyjamas, blue and white stripes, met him at the door. Unless this was the butler, he had hit upon the secret in one bold stroke. Beyond him Carl saw an apartment so sleek and contemporary it made an IBM lobby look eclectic.

'I'm looking for Ted Randall,' said Carl. 'I'm . . .'

'You're Carl Knight!'

'I know,' said Carl.

'I'm Sebastian Smith,' he said, flinging wide the door. 'Come in! This is absolutely marvellous.' Carl stepped in. 'Ted!' Sebastian called. 'You'll never believe who's here. GEN. Carl Knight in person.'

A personal appearance, thought Carl, as opposed to what? Sending an emissary, I suppose. Or a recording.

'But . . .' Sebastian turned to him wonderingly. '*Why* are you here?'

Ted Randall walked out of the bathroom, partly dressed. He stood buttoning his shirt, looking puzzled.

150

'Carl Knight?'

His arms aren't that big, Carl was thinking. They're the most normal-sized arms I ever saw.

'You threatened to murder me last night, remember?'

'I'm terribly sorry,' he said. 'I see my mistake.'

'Ted!' Sebastian looked surprised and pained. 'How could you? You know how I adore his music. Unless'– his face cleared, looked quite dazzled with delight – 'was that why? Were you jealous?'

Ted ignored Sebastian and said to Carl, 'Last night you looked older. I thought you were someone else.' He looked rather disapproving. 'If you're Carl Knight, you're awfully young to be seeing Genevieve.'

'You have a young lover. Why shouldn't she?'

'I'm a man. It's different.'

'I'm a man, too,' said Sebastian. 'And I have an older lover. Much older. Positively decrepit.'

They all laughed.

'I've come,' said Carl, 'so that you'll know not to kill me if Laura gets told.' But, clearly, thought Carl, what Laura mustn't be told is that her father is gay. Now that I've discovered it, I could tell and therefore I'm as vulnerable as Jim. 'I won't tell,' he said.

'You can't tell,' said Ted, 'since you don't know.'

'That's right,' he assured him, seeing he must be humoured. 'Genevieve wouldn't tell me. Even though my life had been threatened I couldn't get it out of her. She'd apparently rather I died than divulge a peep of it.'

'She'd never tell. I trust her absolutely.'

Ted's affable smile disappeared. He went from looking like a successful architect getting dressed for the day to the man who had threatened to murder him last night. He frowned and his arms grew bigger and longer. Carl almost said 'I won't tell' again.

Ted went to his bedroom and returned with a tie, which he put on in front of the hall mirror.

Carl wondered if his personal appearance was over.

Sebastian was looking bewildered. 'Know what?' he
151

asked. 'What is all this about telling and knowing? Why don't I know? We have no secrets from each other, do we? What mustn't Laura be told?'

This is absurd, Carl thought. Can't the fool see that she mustn't be told about him?

'Were you really prepared to murder somebody, Teddy? Who? Why?'

I'm getting out of here, Carl thought. I can't stand seeing someone start acting as I did all last night. His voice is even trembling. I think he is going to cry. At least I didn't cry. Or did I? Yes, I seem to remember that I did. How humiliating. But it was just tears, not racking sobs or anything. I know Sebastian is going to go for the racking sobs.

It's too bad I've upset the boy. I should have been more thoughtful, asked to speak to Ted alone – although that would have upset him more. Laura's right. I'm a crumb. I feel crummy.

'I must be going,' said Carl. 'Just be sure not to murder me if Laura gets told. Gen is lunching with Jim Lasky today and will urge him not to tell, but' – Carl spread his arms – 'you may want to threaten him as you did me, just to be sure. It was very effective.'

'Jim Lasky?'

Carl remembered that Ted hadn't known the name. Oh, lord, now he'd fingered him. Was that crummy? Not too. After all, that was the whole idea of coming here, to tell Ted that he, Carl, wasn't the one, and that Jim was. Wasn't it? He felt confused. Wasn't Carl also the one, now that he knew that Ted was gay? Who cared? Almost everyone was gay now. Ted should just tell Laura himself.

'Wait,' said Ted. 'I'll walk out with you.' He went to the bedroom and returned, carrying a jacket. He put his arm around Sebastian's shoulder and kissed him on the temple. 'I'll call you,' he said. He slipped his wallet in his hip pocket and put on his jacket. 'So, Gen isn't marrying Jim Lasky?'

'No, she broke her engagement. She's in love with me.'

'That bastard. He's just doing it to get a hold on her, then?'

'On who?' Carl asked. 'Gen? Or Laura? Doing what?'

'Never mind.' He glared again. 'Maybe I should see this guy right now. Do you know where he lives?'

'Yes. I'll drive you there, if you like.'

'Let's go.'

'What about me?' Sebastian asked. 'Can't I come?'

'Don't be silly. It's nothing to do with you.'

Carl admired the way Ted treated Sebastian. Gen should treat me like that, he thought.

They went down the steps, out of the door, and into Carl's car.

Ted looked very distinguished, Carl thought. Wilkes Bashford clothes, they looked like. A nice eight-hundred-dollar suit. Although he looked pretty natty himself in his baggy corduroys, espadrilles, and yellow rugby shirt. He rubbed his chin to see if he'd shaved. He hadn't. Jim was also damned distinguished-looking, but maybe he'd look baggy and unshaven when Ted was through with him.

'I wonder what time he leaves for work,' Ted said, as they drove west through the city. It was a sensational San Francisco day. The city looked cloud-white, while the sky and bay, vying for the winning blue, were cleft by the shimmering gold of the Marin Hills.

'Eight thirty,' Carl said.

'How is it you know so much about him?'

'Checking up on the competition. You have to know your enemy. I've been pretty worried about him all along. Still am.'

'He's a man to reckon with.'

'He seems to have a hold on Gen.'

Ted wouldn't be led. Clammed up.

Sometimes it's better for a kid to be told things, Carl would have liked to say. But Ted would not be receptive. My mother was gay, he could go on to explain. How had he felt when he learned that? In a way it had helped him, because he'd never felt she loved him. Learning she was

153

gay seemed to help explain why she didn't, as if not loving him was something she couldn't help. Now he saw that it wasn't true. Still, it had seemed to assuage his forlornness at the time. He had an idea that Ted loved Laura very much.

Carl glanced at Ted. Better not to speak to him at all. He was probably busy working himself up into a murderous wrath. It couldn't be easy to threaten a man with murder – especially so early in the morning.

Ted spoke. 'I still can't get over how much older you looked last night. Your walk . . .'

'Don't you start about my walk,' Carl sighed. 'If you must know, it was because I'd been on a bit of a heroin binge and it temporarily aged me. That's Gen's thesis at any rate. But don't tell Laura. I've got enough trouble about Laura liking me without her learning I've got a monkey. Don't tell Laura or I'll kill you.' Ted didn't smile.

It felt good. He could probably get into murder threats himself, really get a kick out of them. 'I'll kill you if you tell her,' he repeated, deciding he meant it. 'I mean it.'

'All right, all right, I get the message. Why on earth did you just tell me if it matters so much to you?'

'To me it's not such a big deal if I occasionally have a shot of the stuff, but Gen thinks it's Armageddon. As for Laura, I can't seem to persuade her that I won't ruin her mother's life just by my very nature. Laura and Gen are so close.'

'That's an understatement.'

'I want to be that close to Gen,' Carl said sadly.

Ted smiled. 'Good luck.' They were quiet and then Ted said seriously. 'I'm sure it's very worrying to Gen, the heroin. It's not that she'd disapprove so much as be scared about it for you.'

'Yes, I'm going to give it up. If Gen comes to live with me I'm going to quit. But I can't tell her that. I want her to come on her own, not just to save my life, although blackmail's not at all beneath me. I'll do anything to win her.'

154

Carl suddenly perked up. 'Here we are,' he said excitedly, 'and that's him coming out of the house now. He walks to work.'

Carl pulled up abreast of Jim and Ted leapt from the car. He grabbed Jim by the arm. 'My name is Ted Randall,' he said.

'Yes?'

'I just have one thing to say, and that is that I'm going to kill you if you tell Laura.'

'You're threatening me?'

'Yes.'

Carl was bitterly disappointed. It wasn't anywhere near as good a threat as he'd had. I mean, what kind of threat is it, he wondered, if the object had to *ask* if it's a threat? And Ted didn't even hurt his throat. There was no terror involved, no approach from behind, no surprise, no moon. It was the most pathetic murder threat he'd ever seen. He could have done much better – even with his slight stature, flab, and English accent. Carl felt like weeping with disappointment.

'Thank you,' Jim was saying. (Thank you! That's the kind of threat it was. He was thanking him for it!) 'I'll bear this in mind when I make my final decision.' He walked away. A cool customer. Very cool, these recombinant DNA boys. Carl was abashed. He himself had shouted cravenly after Ted, *I won't. I won't tell Laura!*

'I am so disappointed in you,' Carl wailed when Ted came back to the car. 'You didn't scare him at all. Not one bit. All he's going to do with your threat is bear it in mind. And that's all it was worth, I can tell you. What happened? Your attack on me last night was masterful. I practically peed in my pants.'

'There's something sort of commanding about him,' Ted admitted. 'Once I was eye to eye with him, I wilted. You're right. It wasn't very effective. God, if only you knew how I hate that man. Always have.'

Always? What's this about always? Carl wondered. Well, I'll come back to it. 'I hate him, too,' he said. 'Laura

155

really wants her mother to marry the scumbag.'

'She does?'

'Yes. If only we could show Laura what a bastard he is.'

But was he a bastard? Maybe he wasn't. Maybe he was a better man than either Ted or Carl. What an appalling thought. 'Look,' he said, 'why don't you return tonight when the moon's up and give him the real treatment. I'll come, too. We could both jump him.'

'This isn't a game,' Ted said angrily. 'You're treating it like a game. This is important to me.' Tears came to his eyes. He roughly wiped them away.

'I know! I know!' said Carl hastily.

'You don't know,' Ted growled.

'Right. I don't know.'

After a few minutes, Ted said, rather uneasily, 'Did you notice that Sebastian followed us?'

'No,' said Carl, not really interested and priding himself on the fact that he had never yet followed Gen. He was bound to in time, so he might as well feel proud while he could. 'I wonder how he got out of his pyjamas so fast?'

'Oh, he's very accomplished,' Ted said, half in pride, half in despair. 'When it has anything to do with me, his powers become almost supernatural.'

Carl drove Ted to his office in downtown San Francisco. Then, instead of going home, he drove on to the medical centre to see Jim Lasky himself. Not to threaten him, or jump him, just to talk to him. He figured the matter was still in his hands and he should keep on with it, conclude it.

9

'So,' said Jim, sitting down to lunch with Gen. 'My daughter has been raised by a fruit. That's just great.'

They were at the Cliff House, from where one was supposed to view sea lions disporting themselves in Pacific breakers but never did.

'What's this?' Gen asked, looking at Jim with a feeling of revulsion, thinking how she hated him, wondering why she'd never seen what a son of a bitch he was. Love is blind, that's all. Love is blind, as the poet said, and lovers cannot see. And one's first love has such a lifelong hold on one, an historical hold.

'I've learned that Ted Randall's gay. Your friend Carl Knight told me. He came to tell me that Ted had threatened him with murder if I told Laura. He thought he'd pass on the threat since it was intended for me. No need, actually, since Ted came earlier this morning and threatened me in person.'

Jim buttered a roll, bit and chewed. Gen looked out of the window at the sea lion-less sea, thinking, Carl must have visited Ted, then gone to see Jim. He has been busy. But towards what end? Couldn't he trust me to see that Ted wouldn't murder him? she thought, rather crossly.

'Carl went on to tell me that he knows what the secret is – Ted Randall's being gay. I think I managed not to show how stunned I was at the news. He then told me to mind my own business and not meddle in your life, since I am no longer your fiancé. He doesn't want me distressing you or Laura. The man, needless to say, is terribly confused. I, however, have been enlightened. It is more important than ever now that Laura should know the truth about her birth, so she'll know her real father isn't a pervert.'

'Do you wish to order now?' the waiter inquired. How

long had he been standing there?

Jim ordered fish for them both. Gen waited for the waiter, who was gay, to go away before saying, through clenched teeth, 'Gays are not perverts.'

'Do you think what they do is natural? Do you think that is any way to live? Do you think they are well, happy people? I am horrified and disgusted. I can't believe you've kept this from me all these years.'

'For one thing, you weren't in the least interested in Laura until recently. For another, I only learned about Ted four days ago. He only realized it about himself after we were separated. Until the age of fifteen, Laura was raised by parents who loved her very much and who had a stable relationship. Laura has known about Ted for some years, but she never told me. I wish she had. It would have helped me understand myself better. But the situation between me and Ted was such that she never relayed any information about one of us to the other. Again, you are displaying unconscionable prejudice and a lack of tolerance and understanding. I thank God I learned this about you in time. I really don't want to stay and eat with you.' Gen rose to her feet.

'Very well. I am going to tell Laura the truth and you can't stop me.'

Gen was having difficulty in breathing, let alone speaking, and all she wanted to do was leave, but she felt she had to speak for Ted. 'Think of Ted,' she said. 'He really does love Laura much more than you do. He doesn't want her loyalties torn. He doesn't want to lose her. He wants to have grandchildren. And that's something you don't want from Laura, since they'll all be black. I don't see what you gain.'

'She should know the truth,' he said doggedly.

'This has all got so out of hand, I can't believe it!'

'If you hadn't met Carl Knight. . .'

'If? A scientist should know better than to say if. What is, is.'

'And Laura *is* my daughter.'

158

Gen departed, temper high. She turned on her heel and almost ran. She passed their waiter who, confused, said, 'You're going?'

It was only when she was in the car and her five senses were in working order again, along with her breathing apparatus, that she realized the waiter was Sebastian Smith.

10

In the end, Gen thought, while working out on the Nautalis machine at Carl's, I have the power. Only the mother can say who the father is. I could swear to Laura it was Ted, if I chose. But where are my loyalties? Not with Jim or with Ted. Only with Laura. I have some sympathy for both men. I can see both their points of view. But it is as if Laura were a piece of property to which both men want the title. She's mine, they're both saying. I want her. But she's not theirs. She's not mine either, or anyone's. She's her own woman: a grown, mature, lovely person, in love with a man whom neither Jim nor Ted even knows, to whom she will devote herself from now on.

What if Jim does tell her and she comes to me for corroboration and I am forced to say which it is. What shall I say?

Rick came to the door of Carl's makeshift gym. 'Your daughter's here. I put her in the living-room.'

Gen took off her wet T-shirt and pulled on a grey sweatsuit. As she walked into the living-room from the front hall, Carl entered from the studio beyond. She kissed Laura, then Carl.

'I've just come from Jim,' Laura said.

'Did Jim . . . tell you?' Gen asked, feeling suddenly weepy and shaken and surprised to be so affected, and to feel so useless and hopeless and as if she'd somehow, long

159

ago, let Laura down. (Oh, daughter of my womb who suckled my breasts, little daughter now grown to woman, forgive me if I've done you wrong.)

'Yes, he told me.'

Carl, seeing Gen fall apart, wanted to help. He put his arm round her, stood protectively by. 'Listen to me a minute, Laura,' Carl said. 'I don't want to meddle, but I think I can help. You see, my mother was – is – gay.'

Laura looked at Carl and frowned, while Gen said, 'Oh, dear.'

'I was only about eleven when I found out. My father brought me up. She went off and married a woman.' He would have to start lying here. He couldn't say how glad he was to understand why she had hated him, why she had deserted him. 'She loved me and wanted to be with me but her lover stopped her. Her being gay didn't make her love me less, not at all. She was still my mother.' What am I saying? he wondered. What point am I trying to make? He blundered on. 'You're still every bit Ted's daughter – just as if he were heterosexual. More.' Why more? 'I wish my mother loved me as much as he loves you.' That part was true enough.

'Carl,' said Gen gently, but with some exasperation, too. 'That's not it. Laura knows Ted's gay. She has for years. She understands about it and it doesn't matter.'

Carl felt extremely embarrassed. He wished a hole would open up in the rug and swallow him.

'What is it? What did Jim tell her, then?'

'He told me he was my real father,' said Laura to her mother as if Carl weren't there, as if indeed he had been swallowed by the rug. 'He told me you'd been lovers twenty years ago and that you got pregnant by him. He couldn't marry you so you married Ted. Ted made you promise never to tell me he wasn't my father. Now Jim feels I should know the truth. Is it the truth?'

'Yes,' Gen said. 'It is.'

'Jim said you'd always loved him, that you'd really been waiting for him all these years, that you divorced

160

Ted when he came here to San Francisco and found you, and that as soon as his wife died and he was free at last he asked you to marry him so that we three could finally be the family we were meant to be.'

'You've loved Jim for twenty years!' Carl exclaimed. 'Where do I come in? I don't understand. Laura isn't the only one who wasn't told.'

'He also told me you're a junkie,' said Laura, turning to him. Apparently he'd been regurgitated by the rug and admitted to her presence.

'He is not!' Gen cried. 'What a thing to say. It's totally untrue. And that's not all that's untrue,' she added grimly.

'Jim said you almost died from an overdose only a little while ago, *since you met Mom*. I don't know if Mom knows this. I certainly didn't and Mom tells me everything. Well, unless she's promised not to, she does.'

Carl felt he had nothing left. First he'd babbled about his gay mother when it wasn't at all to the point. Then he'd learned about this undying love affair of which Laura was the offspring, making him feel like a pawn in a game he didn't know was being played. Finally, his lover's daughter had called him a junkie.

Not a genius.

Not an artist, not a man, not a lover – a junkie. A cipher. A burnt-out subhuman, beneath contempt.

And that was how he felt. He couldn't remember he was the other things. If Gen didn't love him and was going to marry Jim, that was all he was, a junkie. That was what he would be from now on.

'I have to go now,' he said. 'I don't belong with the two of you any more. I'm leaving. Goodbye, Gen. Goodbye, Laura. You're right. You're right about everything. The truth has come out. Three cheers for the truth. I wish you all the best. Goodbye.'

Gen did not understand. She was too concerned about Laura and what she was feeling, how she was handling the knowledge she'd had thrust upon her. Her attention was

161

not on Carl.

She heard him say goodbye, saw him leave the room, but it didn't register.

Then, alone in the room with Laura, both of them silent, she heard again Carl's 'I have to go now. Goodbye'. She was reminded of the night on the yacht and her departure then, feeling as if a bomb had exploded inside her and that she must make a gigantic effort to hold herself together or fly apart in a million fragments. She must go after Carl at once – as he had come after her. She jumped up, ran to the door, opened it. 'Carl, wait!'

'Mom! Where are you going? Aren't you going to talk to me? You haven't said anything. Mom, I need you now. You can talk to Carl later. Please!'

Torn! torn! One part of her strained after Carl, the other was held fast by Laura. True, she could talk to him later. He'd be here, in his house. It would be all right.

'Mom?'

She turned from the door, saying sadly, 'You shouldn't have called him a junkie. That hurt him.'

'I'll apologize. I will. I didn't mean it the way it sounded. I was quoting Jim, who doesn't understand that most musicians use drugs, that it's part of the scene. I'm sure it worries you a lot. Carl was sweet, really, telling me about his mother.'

Gen smiled. 'Oh, Laura, he's the sweetest man. In time you'll come to know it and to see how good he is, how kind. Meanwhile' – she took Laura's hands in hers and they sat down together on the green sofa – 'let me tell you, as best I can, about Jim, Ted, me, and you.'

This took almost an hour. When she was done, Carl was gone.

FOUR

1

Carl heard Gen call, 'Wait!' and accordingly waited, stopped dead in his tracks in the hall at the bottom of the stairs. Full of hope, he waited for her rush towards him, for the encircling arms that would assure him he was loved, was somebody. But she didn't come, in a rush or at all. He turned, saw her standing hesitantly in the door, head turned not towards him but away. Then her body went the way of her head and she was no longer in the doorway. Still he waited. She had commanded him to wait, had she not? Still she did not come. He began to walk again, dragging his feet up the curving staircase, slow motion, giving her a last chance to appear before he disappeared. Dismally he went along to his bedroom, collected his wallet and leather jacket, then sought out Rick in his suite of rooms on the second floor where he was lying on his bed reading *Don Quixote* for about the thirteenth time.

He looked up from the book to the wretched face of his friend.

'I'm going away,' Carl said hollowly.

'Oh yeah? Where?'

'I don't know. You may have to cancel the Japanese tour.'

'Do you want to talk about it?'

'No.'

'You've told Gen?'

'No. She's busy having an immortal love affair. She's trying for the Guinness Book of Records – it's that long and lasting.'

'When will you be back?'

'Don't hold your breath.' Carl turned to go.

'Don't lose yours.'

'What?' He looked back.

'Don't lose your breath. You need it to play with and to live with. Take care of yourself and your beautiful breath, OK, baby? For the sake of your public and friends.'

'How nice.' Carl managed a wintry smile. 'You make me sound like a person.'

When Gen, with Laura, came looking for Carl and found Rick, Rick repeated their elliptical conversation.

To all her questions he could only reply that he knew no more than Carl had told him. No, Carl had never done this before. Yes, he looked shaken and unhappy. Gen knew how sensitive he was. Yes, he would contact her as soon as he heard anything, although she would probably hear before he did.

The unsaid word was heroin. Gen was terrified that Carl was off on another binge, and this one not in the shelter of his home under the loving eyes of Rick. Her lips trembled with the desire to ask who Carl's contact for the drug might be, but she could not bring herself to do so. If Rick knew, and if he were as frightened as she was, he would investigate himself. She felt it would humiliate Carl if she were to track him down that way. In any case, if he chose to go off for a time, it was not appropriate for her to go chasing after him like a felon.

Laura had hurt him and she had failed him. All she could do now was wait patiently for his return.

No, there was one other thing she could do, one form of action she could take that would make her feel less help-less.

Saying a hasty goodbye to Rick and Laura, she left the mansion and drove to Jim's house. John, a Filipino whom Jim hired on special occasions, opened the door. Gen remembered that Jim was having a reception this after-noon for Francis Crick of *The Double Helix* fame.

She was still in her grey sweatsuit and John looked scandalized. Not a chic sweatsuit, it was the kind you buy at an army surplus store and put on after pumping iron to

166

sop up the sweat and keep off the chill. 'Has it begun?' she asked.

'Another few minutes and people should start to arrive,' John said. 'You have just time to change.'

Gen strode past him to the living-room. Everything was sparkling. Flowers adorned every table. Hors d'oeuvres patterned the silver trays. The bar was spangled with glasses and bottles and buckets of ice.

Jim stood at the far end of the room, sartorially splendid. He looked pleased with himself. Here was a man, it seemed to her, who never questioned. Anything he did was OK simply by virtue of his being the one who did it.

'Gen!'

'You rat!'

'Why? I told you I was going to tell her.'

'And I told you you had no right to. You have meddled in my life.'

'Now, take it easy. People will be arriving any moment.'

'And I should quietly drift away and not cause any trouble. Just as I did when I was carrying your child. What a good girl I was not to cause any fuss but to slink away and find some poor chump to play the father until it suited you to lay claim to your daughter. And why does it suit you now? For no reason I can see except to meddle in my life and Laura's and show yourself to be the rat you are.'

All this erupted from Gen in loud jerky phrases and it was a marvel how little effect it had on Jim. He seemd to be giving her half an ear, the other half alert to the doorbell, and the rest of his attention being given to checking that the party arrangements were complete. He was actually rearranging some of the canapes, then standing back to observe the effect.

He doesn't care, Gen thought. He's got what he wants. Even if I told him, which I never would in a million years, that poor Carl has gone off the deep end, he wouldn't care in the least. He'd go to the door to greet his guests, urbane as all hell.

167

Although she'd stopped talking, he neither answered nor deigned to notice her, but instead continued his inspection, now lifting the bucket top to check the ice.

Enraged, Gen grabbed the bucket from under the lifted top and emptied it over his head. That was enough to get his attention, although getting his attention wasn't what she wanted now. She wanted to kill him. The ice cubes rebounded and splattered about the rug and table. She came after him, swinging the heavy silver bucket, going for his head.

'Gen! Good God! Stop!' He ran from her, a crouched run, his hands over his head as if expecting another rain of cubes. She ran after him, swung the bucket back to wing it at his head, but at that moment slipped on the ice and went down.

John appeared at the living-room door, a picture of consternation. The doorbell rang and he turned to answer it. Jim crunched across the rug to Gen and helped her to her feet. The fall had jarred her. What a relief it would be to burst into tears, she thought. Making a gigantic effort not to, she didn't.

Instead she said quietly, despairingly, in a trembling voice, 'I hate you so much.'

She knew that the hatred she'd felt towards Ted and the five years of silence she'd kept on the strength of it were only a prelude to what she now began to feel for Jim. That had just been beginner's hatred, a tyro silence. With Jim she would master the feeling and the treatment, the silence being periodically broken by fits of violence. Eventually she would be able to give courses in the art. And if she had truly lost Carl because of Jim . . .

John ushered in three scientists: Francis Crick, looking sensational, and Bruce and Giovanna Ames. Bruce was a favourite of Gen's. It was he who had developed a test to discover carcinogens in everything under the sun from hair dye to pyjamas. Now he was deep in a study of rancidity, to see if it might be Ariadne's thread out of the labyrinth of cancer's cause and cure.

No one paid particular attention to her sweatsuit, which was one of the nice things about scientists, but they did seem rather surprised by the ice cubes scattered higgledy-piggledy all over the rug. 'Be careful where you step,' Jim said, after greeting them (urbanely). 'We've had a little accident here.'

The doorbell rang clamorously as more people arrived.

Gen looked at Jim. Her anger had dissipated now, was draining away from her, leaving her dizzy and trembling. What should she say? Last words to the love of her life, now the hate of it.

'I'm sorry.'

Why did she say that? Of all things! What did she mean by it? Was it just her training in civility reasserting itself after the minutes of primitive regression? Did she mean, I'm sorry for the mess I made of your living-room before this important party? It was nothing compared with the mess he'd made of her life! Was she sorry it had all ended so hideously, sorry she'd behaved like an idiot, or sorry that she'd almost done him real harm? Which she had. That's why she was trembling. She really had almost bashed his head to a bloody pulp. That had been her intention. Imagine! All these people might have arrived to find a murdered host and she, as a result, might have been imprisoned for life. Still, if she had lost Carl, she might as well be. This thought required another gigantic effort not to cry.

'Gen has to be going,' he said to the Ameses, and to others who were entering. 'Too bad.'

Everyone expressed dismay. Gen smiled feebly and tottered away

'How about if everyone just grabs up an ice cube and throws it in the fire,' Jim suggested merrily. 'No putting them down each other's necks, now.'

Gen sat for a while in her car until the trembling subsided. What had she accomplished? Nothing. She'd given Jim a moment's unease from which he quickly recovered. Carl was gone. She'd not been there for him when he most

169

needed to be reassured. Instead, she'd helped Laura through her bad time. That was good. Laura was coping and for the time being she wasn't going to tell Ted what she had learned. Maybe she would never tell him. What Laura still didn't know was that her true father was a prejudiced son of a bitch and that Carl was a prince and a sweetheart. These things could not be told to Laura, only learned by her in time. Only facts could be told and facts were nothing.

Gen started the car, engaged the gear, and slowly pulled away. She would go back to *Loiter Longer* now and wait for Carl. That would be her life now. There was nothing more important. And somehow, by the very strength of her waiting, she would keep him from harm, and by the strength of her longing, hasten his return.

2

Gen settled into a state of fear, longing, anguish, apprehension and despair that only deepened as the hours, then days, passed with no word from Carl.

One night, as Carl had originally predicted, she slept with Rick. She wanted the human warmth, the closeness to Carl himself at one remove, to be near his phone in his house with his friend. She didn't want to be with anybody but Rick – even to talk to. To lie all night tucked against his back with her arms around his waist replenished her, allowed her some sleep at last, and therefore gave her the strength to go on waiting.

She wore a granny gown and there was no idea of sex; only love, warmth, and comfort, which Rick generously provided, and needed for himself. He told her that when he was a little boy he would often go to his mother's bed at night and snuggle up to her when he was scared or sad, and fall asleep enveloped in her voluminous warmth.

170

When he became adolescent, she put a stop to it and he missed it sorely. Then, with joy, he realized that he could pretend to sleepwalk to her bed, ostensibly not knowing what he was doing. He would enter her room in the classic manner, arms out, eyes open but unseeing.

She caught on pretty fast and he was banned from her bed for good. He said that sleeping with Gen gave him the same feeling except that she was a lot bonier. They vowed to be mother and son for ever, never to ban each other.

Gen alerted Missing Persons, although Rick advised her not to. Thrice daily she called the Highway Patrol to discover the names of any accident victims. Laura said all the wrong things. 'He is purposely trying to worry you. He is trying to get attention. He was upset by all the business about my father. He just can't bear you to give your love and attention to anyone else, especially me, you know that. You know that's the way he is. It's just emotional blackmail and childish sulking. He'll come home, Mom. Just go on with your life. You haven't even run for three days. Go for a run. It will clear your brain. Stop worrying!'

Of course, Gen did not dare to tell her how mortally afraid she was that Carl was in a coma somewhere, beyond reach, beyond help.

And if, as Laura suggested, Carl was trying to make her realize how much she needed him, he was succeeding. Life without Carl was empty. She could not go on with her life because there seemed to be no life to go on with. Her houseboat, her running, had no substance any more, no reality. Her friends were cardboard figures, cartoon characters, white balloons coming out of their mouths.

This last talk with Laura was on the evening of the fourth day. It was by telephone. Gen was at *Loiter Longer*, Laura at Ted's. Laura is right, Gen decided. I should go for a run. It will return me to myself.

It was after seven when she started. She ran to Mill Valley, to the end of the bike path, and then up Kite Hill, over the Tam High Cross Country course and back to the bike path for the straight shot home. It was raining, which

171

was meteorically unaccountable for August. The rains fell from November to May and the summers were always bone dry. It felt good, however, refreshing. Laura was right. The run was a wonderful idea and she would have a good twelve miles under her belt when she was done. She ran easily, without strain, breathing well. She concentrated on relaxing her shoulders, letting them drop. Anxiety had hoisted them up around her ears. Poor Gen, people must be saying, she was such a good runner before Carl disappeared and she became a hunchback.

By now it was dusk. As she drew near Sausalito, she wondered whether to include the marsh loop. She liked to take it when the tide was low and she could get through the channel. It brought her close to the water line and to the birds which fed on the medley of minute, muddy organisms revealed by the tide: insects, crawfish, minnows and their ilk.

She decided to include it. Although uncertain about the tide, she figured she could always double back if the channel was watered over.

The clay path through the marsh grass was not much wider than her footmark and rolled up and down in little heaves of the earth as if the path had solidified one day when the marsh was laughing. It was fun to run on, and the ambiguous state of the tide only added to the adventure.

Yes, it was fun, except that tonight it was muddy and slippery because of the freak rain. The mud was hanging on to her shoes, clogging her waffle soles. Carrying more weight was OK, resistance training, but her feet were losing their grip on the ground. A couple of times she slipped and almost fell. She should have realized that her shoes were trying to tell her something and stopped running then and there, but she didn't. It only added to the fun – racing along the ribbon of path, along a tiny isthmus, slipping and sliding, winging it, the day fighting off the coming night and losing, the glimmering water and, yes, the sea birds, suddenly manifesting themselves at her

172

approach, whole flocks of sandpipers bursting into flight, rupturing the air. One lone bird, a great blue heron, rose up on fabulous wings, seemingly in slow motion, as if to show the sandpipers how taking to the air should be done – tranquilly and with nonchalance.

Gen wished she could recognize birds by name, song, and peep. She knew the heron. She knew that if the bird was white and could strike a knockout pose it was an egret. The way she catalogued the other marsh birds was: little birds were sandpipers, middle-sized ones were curlews or semipalmated plovers (although she had yet to see a middle-sized bird that resembled half a palm tree) and big ones were . . .

Suddenly, one leg slipped and flew up in the air, neither rising slowly like the heron or suddenly like the sandpipers but awkwardly like a leg. The other leg buckled under her and she went down, hearing a most bloodcurdling crack from the location of her ankle. She was down, down in the mud and hurting. 'Oh! Oh!' A thin keening rose into the drizzly darkening air. The marsh moaner. Embarrassed, she subsided to a pathetic whimper.

While she sat in the mud whimpering, and wondering what to do, the ankle got busy. Within seconds it was as big and round as a cantaloup, heading for a honeydew. Broken or sprained, it made no matter. Broken would mean a cast but fast healing. If it were sprained, if the cracking sound had been not a bone but a ligament, it could mean *months* of healing. 'Oh curses!' she said aloud. She tried to quell the stream of tears, more of self-pity than of pain. 'I should never have come. I was happy just sitting around *Loiter Longer* being depressed, and now here I am with a broken ankle and out for the count. It will be months before I run again. No Carl, no running. I might as well die. I probably *will* die, since I can't move. They'll find me in the morning, a pile of bleached bones. I know that sounds like fast work, but nature is wonderful. It has vultures.' She glanced up and there indeed were four or five of the ubiquitous California vulture circling above the

173

marsh – hateful black birds floating on currents of air, having a look around, particularly vigilant when it came to the downed female runner – no mud-bottom minutiae for those suckers.

Gen continued to mutter, biding her time until the ankle reached the honeydew phase, realizing she would have to try to stand regardless. There was no help. Although there would still be people on the bike path at this hour, they were beyond shouting distance, a quarter of a mile away. No one ever took this path but the idiot runner and the occasional idiot birdwatcher. Marshes being without trees, she could not fashion herself a crutch.

She was simply going to have to get up and honeydew it home. And she wouldn't backtrack if the tide was too high. She would ford the channel. She couldn't get more wet and muddy than she already was.

She hoisted herself on to one leg and two hands, paused, then acquired a vertical stance on one leg, heronly. Well, she couldn't walk that way. As she couldn't fly or float, she would now bite the bullet, put down the wounded leg and place weight on it just long enough to move the other foot forward. In this way she would make her way home and so disappoint the trencherman vultures.

3

Gen knew she would make it home when, a mile and a half later, she arrived at the magnificently deteriorating *Charles Van Damme*, a San Francisco Bay ferry boat from the prebridge era, beached all lopsided by the pier, lived in by persons who didn't mind their floors at a thirty-degree angle. Gen, cold and wet, was shaking all over. Her mind was shaking, too. She felt gaga. As she passed through the yard of moribund anchored vehicles where the car people lived, she thought what a good thing it was

174

she was a boat person and not a car person. If her first date with Carl had been dinner in a car, he'd have got quite discouraged about her, not to mention terminally claustrophobic. She began giggling at the thought of Carl arriving at her door only to discover it was a car door. Then her giggling changed to weeping. 'Oh, Carl,' she lamented, 'where are you? Please come home. Please, love, wherever you are, take care of your precious self.'

Why, oh why do I cry so much these day? This crying binge of mine goes on and on. I used to be so tranquil. Tranquil to a fault. I used to be so tough. Now I am absolutely fragile, so fragile my bones are breaking.

She knocked up Ben, as Carl would say, which meant she rang his doorbell. Ben gathered her into his arms and care. He gave her a dry robe to get into, blankets to put over herself, then put on the kettle for tea. Pearl, the good Lord be blessed for small favours, was out.

'It looks like a sprain to me. You couldn't have walked on it if it were broken. Do you want to go to Marin General and have an X-ray to be sure?'

'No.'

'Good. You're better off here, warming up and calming down, than sitting in Emergency waiting to be treated. Also, the first hours are the most important for a sprain. We want to have the leg up, and ice on the ankle every other ten minutes.' So saying, he clamped a bag of ice on her raised ankle, tying it on with a handkerchief.

Presently he brought her a cup of Oolong tea. Great stuff. She could feel new strength coursing through her. 'I sure fooled those vultures,' she said. 'They're still trying to figure how I got out of there instead of lying back and dying of exposure. Imagine how patient you'd have to be to be a vulture, waiting for wounded things to die. Why do you suppose they can't stand the taste of living flesh? How long does the thing have to be dead, I wonder, before they swoop down and raven? Would I have had to be high? High smelling, that is. How soon do you smell dead to a vulture? Maybe very soon.'

175

She stopped. Perhaps she was being tactless and indelicate. Ben, with all the medical specialties to choose from, had selected pathology, so living flesh wasn't his cup of tea either.

'Anyhow, Ben, I'd love to have that kind of patience. Then I could wait peacefully for Carl's return instead of stewing and fretting and being full of worry and fear. I know he loves me and he'll come back to me if he can. I just worry about something happening to him. He's so young and so gifted. He has so much music still to play for the world.' She began to snuffle.

'Now cut that out. You're just all shaken up because of this ankle.'

'Why won't Laura like him, Ben? That's what all the trouble is about.'

'Laura is conservative, and you and Carl are an unconventional couple.'

'She is? We are? What about her and Monti, for heaven's sake? You call that conservative?'

'They are both serious, thoughtful young people, deeply committed to getting an education and bettering the world with it. Comparatively, you and Carl are wild ones and appear to be flamboyantly unsuitable for each other. What she can't see, what nobody can see, even me, is that you and Carl are actually a lot alike.'

'That's right. We have affinity! Two hearts that beat as one! Oh, thank you, Ben. You've put everything in the right perspective. Imagine me not realizing that Laura was conservative and we were flamboyant. I feel so enlightened.'

Alas, just as she was warming up to a good conversation with Ben, enter Pearl.

Pearl was apprised of the circumstances. She nodded, looked Gen over briefly, pursed her lips, disappeared for a minute and returned with a rum bottle. She poured a slug of it into Gen's tea.

'That'll put some colour in your cheeks,' she said.

'Thanks, Pearl.' This woman really does understand

176

nutrition, Gen thought. Imagine my not giving her credit. Why, she's an outstanding nutritionist!

'I couldn't help but overhear your conversation,' Pearl said.

Listening at the door, Gen thought.

'And I think it's only fair, Ben, to add that just because Laura disapproves of Carl Knight, it doesn't mean she isn't right about him. I think the entire community here feels that Gen could do a lot better, and she's just in for a lot of grief with that young man. Some of which she's experiencing now.'

It wasn't the rum putting the colour in Gen's cheeks. She was furious. But, for Ben's sake she didn't remonstrate.

'Of course,' Pearl continued smoothly, mean as nails, 'water finds its own level. People tend to glorify you, Gen, but I say those that want to be with scum are scum.'

Scum! Gen struggled up from her prone position.

'They glorify Gen because she's glorious,' said Ben loyally.

'Whatever happens,' Pearl went on in her placid, insidious way, 'we'll just have to hope you can keep the car. Then all will not have been lost. You could live for four years on what that car will bring.'

Gen, speechless with fury, looked at Ben to see if he could possibly still think Pearl was 'wonderful'. He looked complaisant. Maybe he just heard the tone, which was pleasant, and paid no heed to the import. This woman was poison. Pure effluvium. Talk about scum!

'I've got to get back to my place now,' she said, the words coming out stiffly. She got up on one leg, also stiffly. 'Thanks, Ben, for your care.'

'You keep on with the ice. I'll have another look at it in the morning. Can you make it all right?'

'Yes, I'm OK.'

Gen limped next door, let herself in. She noticed that someone had taken down Old Glory, wondered who. She flicked on the light and went through to her bedroom to replace Ben's robe with her own. There on the bed was Carl, fast asleep.

'Oh, Carl! Carl!' she cried happily, and fell on to the bed beside him, folding him in her arms. 'My darling! Dearest darling of my heart, you've come home to me.'

He did not respond. She could not wake him up.

4

Four days before, Carl had walked out of his house and gone straight to the airport. He had some idea of going back to England, to the source of his life and of his love for Gen; some idea of finding himself – if he was anywhere at all to be found.

Instead he bought a ticket to New York. First he would go and see Monti. He'd seen Monti's address on a letter to Laura one day when he'd been snooping around *Loiter Longer* and he remembered it, as he remembered all things. He didn't read the letter. He was not that kind of snoop, not the really loathsome kind. (Also, on that particular snooping sortie, he had found a pressed yellow rose!)

He was able to get on a flight right away and, six hours later, he was with Monti. He gave no reason for his sudden appearance and Monti asked for none, seemed to accept that he had run into him one day in New York, just as he had in London.

Carl asked nothing of Monti, nor did he tell him his problems with Laura. Instead, he imbibed of his personality, his clear, astonishing intelligence, his personal elegance, the music of his voice. He was refreshed by, if nothing else, his phrasing. After five hours together, he went away replenished and inspired.

But he did not return to San Francisco, he flew on to London. The plane, Heathrow, the tube station, the Piccadilly line, Kensington, Russell Square, Buckingham

Palace where he'd seen Monti and Gen running by the Palace Guard. What a sight that had been, the fleet and the totally immobile, the black and white runners against the red and black petrified men.

Carl journeyed on to Winchester, to the cathedral, to find the statue of their hero, William Walker the diver, and pay obeisance to it. He almost looked in vain. It was the tiniest statue of anyone he'd ever seen. It was more like a figurine, placed in the darkest apse between the chantries of prelates. It seemd to Carl that William Walker, who saved the cathedral with his own bare hands, was given short shrift in the place that would not still be standing were it not for him. Nevertheless, the humble diver would probably be pleased as punch.

He wandered around the cathedral, looking at graves, windows, statues, memorials. Something held him there. He would almost leave, even be at the door, then he'd be pulled back in, almost as if someone had grabbed his arm.

Finally, fatigued, he sat down in a pew. Shortly after that, he slipped to his knees, clasped his hands, and bent his head. There, in that position, he remained for a long, long time.

Then the cathedral let him go.

Onwards he travelled to Jane Austen's house in Chawton. 'Jane Austen lived here from 1809–1817 and hence all her works were sent into the world. Her admirers in this country and in America have united to erect this tablet. Such art as hers/Can never grow old.'

At last he ended up at his Aunt Fanny's house where, amid her eternal Airedales, he talked with her about his youth, his present self, his art and whether it would grow old, whether it perhaps already had, and his love.

He thought maybe he would give up the concert scene for a while and go away to practise, not just his music but his life; go away somewhere for a time with Gen if she would have him, and begin again, as greenhorn, with the mind and humility of a child, to learn to love and play. 'Except ye become as little children, ye shall not enter into

179

the kingdom of heaven.'

On the flight back to San Francisco, fourteen hours, he remembered that Ted had been going to kill Jim if Jim told Laura, and that Jim had told Laura.

Did this mean that the man was dead? Probably not. He hoped not. Glad as he would be to have Jim out of the way, and his hold on Gen relaxed permanently, it would be too bad for Ted, whom he liked, to do something so extreme and suffer the consequences, which could be quite nasty.

'Once I was eye to eye with him, I wilted,' Ted had confessed. If he wilted during the simple threatening process, chances were he would not be too staunch at the actual murder. Especially as Carl himself would not be there to buoy him up and encourage him.

While thinking these thoughts, Carl asked a stewardess to bring him the American papers of the last few days. He ranged through them in search of the words: *Noted Scientist Found Slain*, but found them not.

He was half relieved, half disappointed. How could Ted have let everyone down so? Didn't he realize that if he didn't follow his threats through he would lose all future credibility? From now on people would laugh in his face when he threatened them with murder.

Carl himself had believed him completely. No idle threatener he, Carl had reasoned. This man means business.

In spite of himself, Carl became gloomy. If Ted had not killed Jim as promised, it was going to be much harder to get Gen to marry him. Twenty years she'd loved the man and he was the father of her beloved Laura. She'd waited all these years for him to be free and now he was free. What could he do? How could he combat all that history? If she would only consent to spend a little time living with him she would see how inseparable they were.

He cheered up as he conceived a plan whereby Gen would have no choice but to accept him. It would take some orchestration but that was what he was good at.

By the time Carl arrived at *Loiter Longer*, except for

catnaps here and there on planes or trains, he had not slept for four days.

5

Gen, unable to rouse Carl, catapulted off the bed and, like a crazed wind-up toy, limped rapidly next door to fetch Ben, crying 'Coma! Coma! Help!', feeling that all her worst fears had been realized. Ben came calmly with his black bag, went to the bedroom, ordered Gen not to hover, and went to work with stethoscope and common sense. He listened to Carl's heart and lungs. He lifted his eyelids to look at his pupils, palpated his skull, pricked him with a pin, then turned to Gen and solemnly pronounced Carl to be asleep.

'Asleep?' Gen echoed numbly.

'He's exhausted, but sleeping normally, not drugged or concussed and certainly not comatose. Just dead tired.'

After Ben had left and Gen had enjoyed her flood of relief and her joy at Carl's safe return, she began (yea, it is ever thus) to get angry. She found herself gradually becoming very cross and sulky. What if Ben hadn't been available and I'd thought Carl was in a coma or even dead and went away and killed myself? It's happened lots of times. Maddened by grief and confusion you have to lash out at someone. God being out of reach, you turn on yourself, just as Juliet did when she found Romeo drugged in a seeming death.

Gen, who wasn't quite herself, what with her sprained ankle and the enormous release from strain caused by Carl's return, now fell into a nervous fit which caused her to wish that she had killed herself instead of calling Ben. Then Carl, upon awakening, would find her all bloody by his side, a knife rising steeply from her snow-white bosom, and learn what a cad he was to go away and frighten her so badly and come back to frighten her worse.

181

But what if he didn't try to kill himself in an ensuing melancholy but instead went to fetch the morning paper and have a cup of coffee at the nearby Café Trieste?

Never mind. Calm down. Be glad he's home, you idiot. Also, think of your ankle. How can you create a convincing death scene and ice your ankle too?

With her fit over with, her heart lightened, began to sing. Carl was home! Home safe. It occurred to her to call Rick. 'He's home,' she said, 'and fast asleep. He looks simply beautiful.'

The next morning, Carl and Gen woke up together tangled tight in each other's arms and legs.

What woke them was Ben bursting into their bedroom, brandishing the morning paper. 'Sorry to startle you. I thought you should see the news at once. I'm off. See you later. You both look OK, I'm glad to see,' and out he went.

Carl and Gen had untangled enough to sit up in bed upon Ben's arrival. He'd put the paper down on their laps. They still had not spoken to each other, had not said hello, goodnight, or good morning, but they hadn't let go of each other the whole night long and sat now with their inside arms around each other and the outside ones holding hands.

The headlines said, *Noted Scientist Found Dead.*

Tightening their holds on each other, they bent their heads to the article. Jim Lasky had been found dead at ten o'clock last night. The time of death was between 7.30 and 8.30 p.m. Cause of death would wait upon the autopsy but he had been badly beaten. According to his houseboy he had received a murder threat within the last week.

The article went on to number his accomplishments, more of which could be found in the obituary on page 30.

Strangely, when Carl and Gen turned to each other for the first time, they spoke of other things, as if to clear the way for the absorption of this news. Simultaneously, they

182

spoke:

'Where have you been?'

'Will you marry me?'

And as simultaneously answered:

'England.'

'Marry?'

Then Gen snatched up the paper, saying, 'This is awful,' and put it down again, staring first out to space and then at Carl.

'Yes, it must be awful for you. It's rather splendid for me actually, since you're now free to marry me.' But his voice was hollow. A man had died. Gen's lover.

'I was already perfectly free. He need not have died.'

Life returned to Carl's voice as he reminded her, 'Laura said you loved him for twenty years!'

'That was all poppycock. You could have waited to hear my side instead of going to England. Why England? Oh, Carl!' She threw herself into his arms. 'Please, please, don't ever go away like that again. I've been so frightened. Ow!' She screamed.

'What? What is it?' he asked, terrified.

'My ankle. I forgot about my ankle. I sprained it last night. You just kicked it by mistake.' She threw off the covers to display the horrid blue swollen thing.

Carl looked sickened. 'I can't marry a deformed person.'

'How can you even talk of marriage with poor Jim dead?'

'That's *why* I can.'

Again she took up the paper as if she could wrest some answers from it. 'Let me read this again. But first, how are you?'

'Fine, thank you, and you?'

She told him how she'd thought he was in a heroin coma, and how she'd gone running to Ben.

'O woman of little faith,' he accused her.

'Why on earth should I have faith?' she expostulated. 'Give me one reason. One!'

183

They were still holding on to each other with all their might.

Carl told her all about his plan to go away with her and start life anew. 'I'm going to begin everything again: our love affair, my music, and my life. It's called Operation Greenhorn and it excludes heroin, forbids it. It's proscribed. For both of us. You can't use it either. Will you come?'

'Can I have an occasional glass of Chardonnay?'

'I don't see why not. We won't be too stringent. This isn't a military coup, with curfew from dusk to dawn and looters shot on sight. Hey, we could call our new place *Looter Longer*.'

'Sweetheart, let's not be silly. It's very serious about Jim.'

'For Christ's sweet sake, why won't you just say you'll marry me and be done with it. Then we can go on from there. It's called clearing the decks.'

'I . . . I . . .' she choked.

'I can't *believe* this,' he said. 'What do I have to do? What more can I do?' He let go of her so he could fling his arms around. 'I've gone all the way to England and back in four days,' he said meaninglessly.

'OK, I'll marry you.'

He threw his arms around her and kissed her with all his heart. 'I love you, I love you, I love you,' he said passionately.

She kissed him back. He entered her without more ado. He'd had an erection ever since he woke up and it was high time. But he wasn't going to make love to a woman unless he married her afterwards. That's the kind of man he was.

Later, they lay back in each other's arms in a stupor of happiness, stroking and kissing and telling each other of the misery of their days apart.

Carl had learned exactly how many bags of concrete William Walker had carried during his five years underwater, and how many bricks, and that his diver's dress

184

had weighed nearly two hundred pounds (which Gen already knew), and that, as well as saying he was proud to have taken part in so grand a work, he had said he was confident his work would stand the test of time.

Then Carl expressed his doubts as to whether his own work would stand time's wretched test. Were his songs not frivolous? Did they do anything for the human condition? Show any vision? Make any statement?

'They celebrate life,' said Gen, 'and that is a great deal. You celebrate life. It is a courageous thing to do. It is generous. You make people's hearts sing. You are a cathedral in your own right.'

At this, Carl was silent and deeply moved. She went on talking, ruining the moment. 'As for your flute playing, Jean Claude Killy himself has commended it!'

'Killy is a skier,' Carl said sententiously. 'I think you mean the flautist, Jean Pierre Rompal.'

Gen blushed. 'That's right, I do. I must learn more about music so as to be a good wife for you.'

6

Because of Gen's ankle, Carl made breakfast. The aroma of frying bacon filled the air. As he pottered about in the kitchen area, he thought what a cosy little place *Loiter Longer* was. He remembered how appalled he'd been by it at first – its smallness and flimsiness and the incredible nearness of its neighbours and how he was consequently loth to spend any nights there. Now it seemed much more homey to him than his mansion in the city. Maybe he was just being nostalgic because Operation Greenhorn would take them away.

Gen moved to the sofa to be near him and pored over the newspaper, addressing herself to the tragedy now the decks were cleared.

'Do you feel sad?' Carl asked as he turned the strips of pig.

'I feel shocked more than anything. I feel guilty, too, for some reason, as if I'd been a party to it. . .'

I could have done it, she thought. I might have murdered Jim. Almost did. I came close. Not really. If I'd really wanted to murder him I'd have gone after him with a weapon, not an ice bucket. But maybe this person didn't *mean* to murder him either.

'I'm surprised that he told anyone about the murder threat,' Carl said. 'It means Ted scared him after all. I'd thought it was such a pitiful threat. It's a good thing I didn't threaten him myself or I'd be in this thing up to my ears. But I knew I'd make a botch of it so I got Ted to do it. Come to think of it, that does make me an accessary. I actually fingered him for Ted.' Carl laid the bacon on a paper towel. 'Now I feel as if *I'd* been a party to it. This is getting to be quite a party.'

'Hold on. This is news to me about you and Ted. I didn't know you'd met him. But of course you must have, because you learned that he was gay, then went and told Jim. So much happened just before you left that we never got to talk over. I never even told you about my horrible lunch with Jim – which, come to think of it, Sebastian witnessed. Did you meet Sebastian?'

'Yes. He's the gay give-away.'

'Oh, that coffee smells good.'

Carl poured her out a mug of it.

'But did you actually go with Ted to threaten Jim?'

'Yes. But the threat seemed so pathetic I decided to talk to Jim myself, man to man, not understanding that this don't-tell-Laura business was a lot more serious than Ted's sexual proclivities. I'm sorry I meddled. I'm sorry I disappeared.' He handed her a bacon sandwich as if in recompense.

'No harm done, really,' she assured him vaguely, biting into the sandwich. After a few chews, she said, 'But there was harm done, because that's what determined Jim to go

186

ahead and tell Laura he was her father. He couldn't stand Ted's being a fruit – his word. He wanted her to know what a sterling, normal father she really had.'

'I see. So he told Laura he was her father, then she told you she knew, then she told Ted and Ted followed through. Am I beginning to talk in verse?'

'No.'

'No I'm not talking in verse?'

Gen put down the sandwich and reached her hands to Carl as if he'd suddenly been taken ill. 'You mean all this time, ever since seeing the paper, you've thought Ted killed Jim? He didn't. Even if he knew Jim told, he wouldn't. He's too gentle a person.' Unlike me, she thought, with another stab of guilt.

Carl took umbrage. 'He's not in the least gentle! And he said he would kill Jim if he told and Jim did tell.'

'But Ted doesn't know that he did. *Laura didn't tell him.*'

'What? She didn't?'

'No. She decided to wait. Or maybe never tell him.'

Carl shrugged hugely and looked wildly about. 'She must have changed her mind, then. Ted killed him. I know he did. He meant business. It was not an idle threat. He hated Jim.'

'Look,' Gen said reasonably. 'Someone apparently hit him in anger but he may have died from a heart attack or from hitting his head when he fell. I bet it wasn't a planned murder. I bet someone just got mad at him and . . .' Gen lapsed into guilty silence. 'Maybe we should call Laura and see . . .'

'Well, one thing is certain. Neither Rick nor I hit him. We'd be afraid to hurt our hands.'

'You'd be afraid to hurt your hands,' Gen said in unison. 'That's the difference between musicians and runners. We're not afraid of hurting our feet.'

'So that's how you got that ankle, kicking Jim in the jaw.' Carl spoke jocularly, not in the least accusingly, but, for the first time, he noticed her guilty demeanour.

'No,' she said, 'I didn't kill Jim. But, since you ask . . .

187

did you?'

'No.'

'Because, if Ted didn't . . .'

'Maybe one of us did. I know. It crossed my mind. Not that you did it but that you might think I did. I had a reason and I have no alibi.'

'Neither have I. I was out on the marsh. Nobody saw me for a couple of hours.'

'I wonder if we could make a case for Pearl's having done it.'

Gen laughed. 'Actually, Pearl was coming back from somewhere when I was at Ben's getting my ankle looked at. Then she started being insulting so I left. That was about nine thirty. You were fast asleep. Do you know what time you arrived here?'

'No. Do you think I killed Jim?'

'Of course not.'

Carl flared up. 'Why don't you exclaim what a gentle person I am, then, as you did when you defended Ted? You don't sound anywhere near as sure about me.'

Gen smiled. 'If you were going to hit Jim you'd have done it right away, not waited until you'd been to England and back in four days. In any case, you wouldn't hit him because of your hands. Also, when you get upset you open your hands, not close them, and fling them around as if you're drying them in the air.'

'I am drying them.'

'Whereas I'd hit him. I'd kick him too. I could have got this ankle that way, but I didn't. I think we should trust each other if we're going to get married. It's not very nice to suspect each other of murder or imagine the other's suspecting us.'

'Right. I've been suspecting you ever since you said it wasn't Ted, and I'm sure you suspected me long before that.'

'I was trying not to show that it had crossed my mind. The trouble with us is that I never know when we're joking. Even now we could be joking or dead serious. Shall

188

we swear to each other that we're innocent?'

'No, I think we should trust each other.'

'It's not fair, though,' Gen sighed. 'You're so much harder to trust.'

'You bitch. That's not true. You're *much* harder to trust because you're so secretive.'

'Before we discuss this any more we should check with Laura to see if she did tell Ted.'

'Right. Do.'

7

Gen hesitated to call Laura at Ted's. She never had and she didn't want to begin.

The problem was solved by Laura's walking through the door. She was extremely distressed and threw herself into her mother's arms. Gen screamed because she'd knocked her ankle. She explained, then made room for her daughter on the sofa beside her.

Carl put on the kettle for more coffee. He always felt uncomfortable when Laura found him there in the morning, as if he'd been 'caught sleeping' with her mother. She never greets me, he thought sadly, feeling anew all his wounds about Laura.

As he measured the coffee into the filter paper, his ears pricked up. Laura was saying, 'I had a terrible fight with Jim only minutes before his death. I'm amazed the police haven't come for me already.'

He looked over at the two women. Laura was unusually animated, her colour high. Gen was wide-eyed and listening. Gen, Carl realized, looked old. It wrenched his heart. She was usually in such ebullient health and spirits, eyes sparkling, face aglow, that one never actually saw the lines of age, the life lived, and suffered. Now, with this ankle, and this death . . .

189

'It was awful,' Laura said. 'I was shouting at him at the top of my lungs. Someone must have heard me. I didn't hit him, I promise you, but I'd have liked to. Why didn't you tell me what a monster he is? He wanted me to leave Monti. He said that as my father he had a right to say what he felt. He actually bribed me to leave him. Isn't that nauseating? He doesn't want his gene pool polluted. His sons aren't giving him grandchildren and I'm the only one carrying on the great Lasky strain which would become defiled by Monti's African one. He doesn't want the only remaining Laskys to be black. He sounded so calm and rational, I couldn't believe I was hearing correctly. Then I thought I'd puke. I got rather hysterical, mostly because of the surprise factor. All this time I thought he was so nice. Did you know?'

'I knew. I first learned when I told him about Monti on the phone from London, and that side of him revealed itself more and more. That's why I couldn't dream of marrying him. Even before I loved Carl, I knew I couldn't. But I couldn't tell you . . .'

'God, and all that time I was wanting you to stick with Jim. Mom . . .' Laura engaged her mother's eyes fiercely. 'Will you please promise from now on to tell me things, no matter what, if they concern me at all?'

'I promise.'

Carl silently applauded. It was a real problem with Gen, keeping things from people, setting herself up as an arbiter of what people should and shouldn't know. Now she had promised to change – at least where Laura was concerned.

So he waited for Gen to follow up her promise by telling Laura she was going to marry him. That certainly concerned Laura to the hilt. But she didn't say a word about it, not a peep.

He handed Laura a cup of coffee and refilled Gen's. He sat on the floor, leaning against the sofa where Gen sat, wondering if he should tell Laura about the engagement. Maybe Gen wanted him to be the one to tell Laura.

190

Gen stroked his hair, not peeping.

Laura suddenly remembered something. She said incredulously, 'Jim told me you'd gone over there and dumped a bucket of ice cubes on his head just before a reception for Crick.'

Carl turned and looked at Gen. 'You did? This is news to me.'

'It was just after you disappeared. I was feeling so upset. And helpless. It was my fault you'd gone, but I had to take it out on someone, I guess. It was awful. I went to his house and, well, like Laura, I went mad. Only I didn't just shout.' She remembered chasing Jim with the bucket, wanting to bash his head in, falling just in time; Jim running, his hands covering his head, fearing further ice cubes, little knowing it was the bucket, now, she had in mind to bounce off his head. Had his murderer chased him in a similar fashion? Or had they grappled and fought? 'Carl, don't look so pleased. It makes me feel you would admire me if I had murdered him – and that you'd expect me to admire you if you had.'

'Your mother and I both suspect each other of the murder,' Carl explained to Laura. 'We don't have alibis. She was alone on the marsh (a likely story) and I was en route from the airport and suspiciously vague about when I arrived here at *Loiter Longer*.'

Gen, in a quavering voice, asked Laura the big question. 'Did you tell Ted you knew Jim was your father?' She and Carl seemed to hold each other's breaths.

'No. That's another thing I fought with Jim about. He wanted me to tell.'

Carl and Gen raised their eyebrows at each other. Ted, seemingly, was off the hook.

While Gen absorbed that information, Carl told Laura about seeing Monti in New York. She hung on his every word. Carl could tell that with Jim out of the way she was more open to him. He felt hopeful. Everything was turning out well. Except for one thing. . .

He turned to Gen. 'Isn't there something you want to

191

tell Laura? Something that concerns her?'

Gen looked bewildered. 'I can't think of anything.'

Carl put his head in his hands and groaned. She'd forgotten she was going to marry him.

He would have spoken, but Sally arrived at that moment and there was a big commotion of greeting. Carl found himself back at his domestic post, putting the kettle on the fire again, this time for tea.

Rick's arrival followed hard on the heels of Sally's. He and Carl greeted each other with intense and loving restraint. Rick was introduced to Sally, and told all about the ankle by Gen. They talked about Jim's death. Laura admitted how close she'd come to striking the fatal blow, something Gen still hadn't confessed. Carl said he'd do anything to get Gen to marry him short of hurting his hand. Having reminded her of their coming nuptials in this oblique fashion, he waited for her to announce their engagement to their *best friends*. However, she didn't.

What was the matter with the woman? He picked her up in his arms and excused himself to the assembly, saying, 'I've got to talk to Gen privately for a minute. Rick, will you finish making Sally's tea and pour yourself some coffee?' He carried her into the bedroom, sliding the door shut behind him with his foot. He sat on the bed with her on his lap and whispered, 'Why don't you tell them we're going to get married? I'm sick of drinking coffee. I want to broach a bottle of Mumms.'

'I . . . I . . . well, it doesn't seem suitable somehow, with Jim not even in his grave yet and both of us under suspicion – by each other, anyhow, if not the police. Shouldn't we wait until it's all cleared up?'

'Are you kidding? It may not be cleared up for years! It could be one of the great unsolved crimes of the century. Or, worse, it could be cleared up right away by their discovering that one of us did it. I wish I knew if you were really on the marsh.'

'But everyone's come to express their dismay over Jim's death. I don't see how we can start drinking champagne

192

and celebrating our engagement. It's horribly inappropriate. It wouldn't look right.'

'To whom?' Carl asked bitterly. 'Pearl?'

'Speaking of Pearl, I think I hear her vicious voice out there now. We'd better rejoin the others. I love you and I do promise you my hand. I'm yours for ever in injuries and in health till death do us part.'

'Death won't part us. I will come, like Orpheus, to get you.'

'I'll be so old and ugly then . . .'

'No. You'll be a sweet old lady. Spry. God, will you be spry! But listen, damn you, you promised Laura you'd tell her everything that concerned her from now on. I think you should at least tell *her* about our engagement.'

Gen looked thoughtful. 'You've got to admit it's hard to tell things. All this time you never told me about your mother leaving you and your father for a woman. I know there's a lot more you haven't told, important things that are difficult to say, even to the one who loves you most.'

'Just answer my question.'

'Yes, I will tell Laura.'

8

Meanwhile, on this day that was one hundred years after William Walker became a qualified diver, a contemporary diver donned a wetsuit, took up his tank, regulator, pressure gauge, fins, booties, weightbelt, hood, snorkel, gloves and screwdriver and, fifteen minutes later, when Carl was bringing Gen back into the living-room to greet Ben and Pearl, slipped into the briny at the end of the pier some ten houseboats down from Gen's. At a depth of six feet or so, he glided through the Richardson Bay water, counting the boats, until he came to hers. Being of an older vintage, it did not float on concrete but on big old sabotageable steel drums.

The diver unscrewed the plugs from these drums. Presently they would fill with water and *Loiter Longer* would begin to sink. When the drums were full, the water would charge on into the hold and thence, bursting open the trap door, into the houseboat itself. *Loiter Longer* would go under until it settled into the mud below. The diver didn't know anyone was on board, although one would have thought that even under water he could have heard the hubbub of voices from the loiterers thereon.

Carl was telling Rick about Operation Greenhorn, a return to ignorance, where, in fact, he had never been. A blissful place, he'd heard it was, from the old saw, ignorance is bliss. He'd experienced bliss with Gen but Rick could have no way of knowing how great sex was with Gen. Or could he?

Ben was wrapping up Gen's ankle so that she could safely hobble about on it. Sally was watching with a keen eye, as she'd wrapped a horse's fetlock earlier that morning.

Laura was telling her mother that she thought she'd take a leaf from Carl's book and disappear, go to New York that very night. That way the police, if they were looking for her, wouldn't find her. Pearl was quiet, trying to eavesdrop on everyone's conversation at once.

Gen told Laura that if the police wanted her they'd think nothing of going to New York to find her. New York was not a sanctuary, not a church. Nor did it, in the spirit of Argentina, feel any qualms about extradition.

But she told Laura not to worry. There was nothing to connect her with Jim. Gen's own connection, however, was well known, and a description of Laura leaving his place after a big argument on the night of the murder could easily pass for a description of herself. It would tie in neatly with the ice cube incident witnessed by John, followed by (she made a clean breast at last, although

194

extremely *sotto voce*) her bucketing after him with intent to kill, Jim scrunching desperately across the rug for his life. Therefore, if they came looking for Laura, she could say it was she who'd been there that night. So she encouraged Laura. 'Good idea. But what about Ted? Won't he be disappointed that you're going away so soon?'

'No, because it turns out that he and Sebastian are leaving for Europe this evening.'

Carl, who, unlike Pearl, could eavesdrop even while talking himself, was doing exactly that. At Laura's statement, his ears pricked up. Oh ho! he thought. Scarpering!

Talk became general as the subject of the murder impinged on everyone's tête-à-têtes. Gen expressed her new idea. 'It will come out about our broken engagement. They will assume Jim broke it off, not I, then they'll hear from John about my fight with him, which,' she muttered hastily, 'was actually a murder attempt, and they will assume Laura's argument was a further fight with me. I don't have an alibi as I was out on the marsh. It's much better they suspect me than Laura.'

'I don't have an alibi either,' said Carl, eagerly following Gen into this new spirit of *wanting* to be a suspect and so showing he'd go to jail for Gen as quickly as she'd go for Laura. (Although he did think it was a bit much her suddenly turning the ice cube dumping into a murder attempt. I mean, really, he thought, murder by ice cubes? Come now.) 'And I have a motive, since I believed Gen still loved Jim and was going to marry him.'

'Oh yes, you have an alibi,' said Pearl. 'Never fear. I can give you one.'

Everyone turned big eyes to Pearl, especially Gen.

Pearl's lips got lost between a smile and a purse as she said, 'I saw you at the Sausalito Food Company last night at the time of the murder.'

Carl flushed with guilt.

'It was between eight and eight thirty,' Pearl went on, 'and you were talking to that little girl who works at the ship's chandler.'

195

Gen turned stricken eyes to Carl. 'You came straight from the airport to her?'

'If he ever went to England at all,' said Pearl, 'which I doubt.'

'Of course I went to England! Would I lie?' he beseeched Gen – stupidly, as who would know better than she what a liar he was? 'Would I lie?' he asked Rick, who was the one person who knew better than Gen he would.

Astonishingly it was Laura who leapt to Carl's defence. 'Of course he wouldn't lie about such a thing. I know he was in New York seeing Monti because, well, because he told me. I believe him. Totally.'

Carl was too deep in the soup to appreciate the fabulous unexpectedness of Laura, his enemy of yore, taking his side. He thought the best thing he could do now was to keep on the subject of whether or not he was in England, so that it wouldn't come back to Dotty. Even now he could feel Gen's wounded-animal eyes on him. 'Proof!' he shouted. 'I have proof. How would I have accumulated all that new information about William Walker, his bricks and blocks and sacks, unless I'd been in Winchester Cathedral and bought the pamphlet about him? Well?'

This threw everyone except Gen into confusion, as none of them belonged to the cult of two who worshipped William Walker. They could make nothing of this cry of bricks and blocks.

Gen said: 'I don't care about England. I just care about the little ship's . . .'

Carl interrupted brusquely. 'Her name is Dotty. It's not nice to refer to her as the little something, as if she were a toy.'

'But why go and see her right away? I don't understand. Here I was, desperately worried . . .'

'Even if he did go to see her before coming to you, what does it matter?' said Rick loyally. 'Why do you have to read something bad into it? It was probably perfectly innocent.'

Everyone remembered Carl's guilty flush.

196

Gen said, 'But . . .'

Rick continued, 'After all, Gen, we spent the whole night together in bed, and that was perfectly innocent. Then you get all upset because Carl was seen talking to a little . . . to Dotty in a public restaurant.'

'Mom!' Laura exclaimed, quite surprised. Gen flushed brightly.

Carl, however, was delighted. 'I knew it. I knew as soon as my back was turned you two would get together. It was written in stone. It was poured in concrete.'

Ben, too, looked pleased. Gen remembered that right from the first Ben had held great hopes for the 'blond-haired fellow'.

Sally looked impressed and Pearl, the trouble-maker, looked as though it was all getting too hard to follow. Laura said, 'I should think you'd be glad he had an alibi, Mom, instead of getting all stupid and jealous because he talked to some little toy . . . I mean, to Dotty.'

'I'm going to call my Aunt Fanny right now and prove I was in England,' said Carl, seizing the telephone to show he meant business.

'Does anyone have the feeling this place is sinking?' Rick asked.

'I do,' said Laura.

'Nonsense,' said Pearl. 'And this call of Carl's is a feint.'

'It does seem lower,' said Gen, still red-faced, and glad of the subject change. 'The view out of the window is different. I wonder if there are too many people on board?'

'Nonsense,' Pearl said again. She was not going to be taken in by the idea of sinking any more than she was by Carl's call to Aunt Fanny.

'Hello, Aunt Fanny?' Carl pretended to have reached her. 'This is Carl. How are you?'

'I doubt with all my heart that he is talking to England,' said Pearl. 'I'll put money on it.'

Carl glared at her. 'A hundred thousand dollars says I am.'

'Done,' said Pearl, shaking his hand, and grimly taking

197

the phone from him.

'Maybe we should get off this thing,' said Rick. There's water coming in. Look.'

'Not until Pearl admits that I'm talking to England and pays through the nose.'

'No! Don't come aboard!' everyone shouted as Ben's three-hundred-pound friend, Arnold, arrived with his chess board and, disregarding the clamour, stepped through the door.

'Hey, what's going on?' Water was splashing around his feet.

'The phone's dead,' said Pearl. 'You're lucky.'

'Abandon ship!' shouted Ben.

'My things!' wailed Gen.

'Women first,' said Pearl, diving efficiently off the back deck.

'No, Arnold first,' said Sally, since he was blocking the door, 'Hurry, everyone!'

Too late.

9

They all ended up in the drink. No one drowned, however, not even Pearl.

Loiter Longer sank to its eaves.

Gen was astounded to discover that Carl couldn't swim. Even inhibited by her ankle, she was able to get him safely ashore, to 'beach him' as she described it later. He didn't flail, which surprised and impressed her since whenever he got upset on dry land he did flail. Only those who jumped off the houseboat from the deck end, Carl, Gen, Pearl and Sally (Pearl swam superbly, unhindered by her high heels and corset), had to flounder in the water. Arnold, Ben, Rick and Laura went out of the front door and were able to grab the dock as the houseboat went down.

The August air was warm and they all dried off in the sun, Ben plying them with Oolong.

Poor Gen could hardly grasp what had happened. Events were following too hard and fast on each other. Within twelve hours she had experienced the ankle, the seeming coma, the murder, the engagement, and now the scuttling of every single thing she owned. Any one of these upheavals, and there was one other nobody knew, would have been enough to last her a decade before she would begin to long for more excitement.

'Look at it this way,' they said. 'You haven't lost everything, you've only got everything wet.'

'That's true.'

'It's all recoverable.'

'How?'

'How what?'

'How will we recover everything?'

'Never mind that now. We will get a winch and hoist *Loiter Longer* up.'

'But how did it happen? How did it sink?'

'I guess there were too many people aboard. Arnold was the last straw. Although it did seem to be going down before Arnold stepped aboard.'

'I do believe there were more people on board at once than there've ever been before, but still . . .'

'It must have sprung a leak.'

'How . . .?'

'Please, no more hows.' This from Carl. 'Come home with me and rest. This has all been too much for you. You still have me and Laura and all your friends.'

'And your car,' said Pearl.

Enfeebled as she was, Gen felt a powerful urge to strangle Pearl there and then, in front of everyone, even Ben. Especially in front of Ben. She was sick of repressing her natural dislike, not to say hatred, of Pearl. She struggled out of her chair to take Pearl by the throat but Carl, reading her mind, held her back.

'If only I could at least run,' Gen said woefully. She began to cry. Her week-long crying binge had still not exhausted itself, and perhaps was still peaking.

'Come on.' Carl carried her, still crying, to the parking lot and the car. 'Have you noticed,' Carl whispered to Laura, 'that your mother goes boohoo when she cries. It's so touching.'

'I know.' Laura giggled. She was walking beside Carl, holding her mother's hand. 'It's just reaction, Mom,' she said comfortingly.

Sally walked along on the other side, patting Gen's back and saying, 'There, there.' Rick brought up the rear with Ben.

They took Gen's car, not Carl's, so she would have something of her own in the city. Laura would drive over with Rick, get her clothes from Ted's house and spend her last night at Carl's.

'Take good care of her!' Laura called to Carl as they drove off. It warmed his heart. It was trusting. It included him. Laura had placed her mother trustingly into his hands.

As they drove out of Sausalito, Gen stopped sniffling and began to study Carl's face. By the time they were on the approach to the bridge, she had decided to speak her mind.

'Remember that night when we went sailing and I got so upset about Dotty and you ended by spending the night with me?'

'It is imprinted for ever on the most battered part of my brain.'

'I remember feeling that you'd somehow orchestrated the whole thing. I have that same feeling now, Carl. I feel as if you've arranged it all so that I'm in your clutches. The man you thought was in your way is dead. Ted is leaving town, so Laura's going away too. My home is deep-sixed and with it all my possessions, including my wallet, so that I have no official identity, even. I can't run. In one fell swoop you have me all to yourself. I'm a prisoner.'

Carl smiled. 'I think you'll be able to drive. The ankle isn't your clutch foot, speaking of clutches, so you'll have that much freedom. You're not a complete prisoner. I meant the marsh to get your clutch foot which is why I didn't buy you an automatic. I thought if I got you an automatic the whole orchestration would go down the drain. I never dreamt the marsh would mess it up and get the wrong ankle. One can't count on a good marsh any more. Marshes aren't what they used to be.'

'Carl, did you?'

'Did I what?'

'Somehow orchestrate this whole incredible débâcle?'

'No, not the *whole* débâcle. Only part of it. I didn't kill Jim. Although I know who did.'

'You do? Who?'

'Wait until we get home. I like to be able to watch your face when we talk.' He handed the man at the toll a dollar and put the car in gear. Before he released the clutch, he said, watching, 'I'll admit to one thing. I did sink your houseboat.'

'Oh!' Gen fainted. He laid her down on the seat with her head in his lap. Poor Gen, he thought. All this is too much for her. It doesn't seem fair. She's so sensitive. She really likes a quiet life. She should never have got involved with someone like me.

He smiled to himself, thinking, she'll cheer up when I explain everything to her, when she sees that it was all for love.

10

'It was all for love,' he explained. Gen was on his sofa,
buoyed up by cushions. One of Carl's entourage had
prepared lunch for them and brought it on trays.

'Also I was gaga, as you would say, from all my travelling without sleep, and so not wholly accountable for my
actions. The plan seemed brilliant at the time. With nowhere to live, you'd come to me. I knew Dotty had a diver
friend so I arranged it with her as soon as I got to
Sausalito, having called her from the airport. I knew
you'd appreciate the beauty of employing a diver to save
our love with his own bare hands. I had to pay him
handsomely. He probably got more for sinking your
houseboat than Walker got for saving the whole
cathedral.

'By morning I'd forgotten all about it, especially when
you agreed to marry me. It wasn't until Pearl blabbed
about seeing me with Dotty that it all came back to me.'

The guilty flush, Gen realized, was about the diver.
And the reason Pearl was so mean about Carl last night
was that she had just seen him with another woman.
Maybe she's not such a bad old crow after all.

'Wasn't that some dive Pearl did?' Carl said. 'I think it
was a swan dive.' He imitated Ben. ' "What a wonderful
woman!" Now it seems crazy that I thought you'd need to
be homeless to love me and come to live with me, but at
the time . . .'

Gen raised herself from her stunned silence to say, 'It *is*
crazy!'

He's crazy, she realized despairingly. He's not a normal
person at all. A normal person would not sink a houseboat. 'It's a terrible thing you've done,' she said. 'I can't
believe it. I think you're so rich that you can't conceive of

202

someone's home and belongings mattering to her. You think she can just buy new ones.'

'Yes.'

'And you're so egomaniacal that you think you can do what you like with people's lives.'

'Yes, that too. Your life, anyhow. But, dearest one, Operation Greenhorn's going to change all that. I'm going to learn not to do terrible unbelievable things. I won't need to do them to get attention. I was just trying to get you to look at me, that's all. The first time I looked at you you covered your face with a blanket. Ever since, I've been trying to remove it.'

'Oh, Carl!' That's so sad, she thought. 'So you sank my houseboat to get me to look at you?'

'Yes. You would never give me your full attention. I had to do something terrible. Or it seemed to me that I did. We're not joking now, are we?'

'No, my darling, we're not.'

'I'm so afraid that you won't marry me now. Will you . . . will you just listen to this song I've written? Please? Before we talk any more.'

'All right.'

'I wrote it the day after we met,' he said, sitting down at the Yamaha. He played the introduction, paused, then began again, playing and singing the lyrics in his own peculiarly sweet and vibrant voice that had set the world on its ear.

> 'I don't know you my darling
> We only just met
> I've loved you for ever
> I'll never forget
> How you looked when we parted
> Our paths only crossed
> Briefly my darling
> Two strangers who paused
> An encounter by chance – two ships in the night
> Crossing and lapped by the waves and the bright
> Rays of the moon on cerulean seas

203

I love you, I want you, I'm down on my knees
I don't know you my darling
We only just met
I've loved you for ever
I'll never forget
How you looked when we parted
A moment to save
You leapt to your feet
I was rocked by your wave.'

When he had finished, Gen held out her arms to him, tears in her eyes. 'It's beautiful. I am honoured. I love that song.' It was true. She felt humbled and blessed. What a gift! What did material things matter compared with love and song? 'Of course I will marry you. You are far more precious to me than any houseboat. Now on to the next catastrophe. Tell me who killed Jim.'

'Sebastian.'

'Of course!'

'When you told me he'd overheard your lunch conversation with Jim, I remembered he'd followed me and Ted on the threatening expedition. Ted told me he was a blue-ribbon meddler. Then, when Laura said he was leaving town, it all fell into place. He might have wanted to kill him to keep him from telling Laura, or because he'd already told. Who knows? Maybe Ted knows or guesses. Or maybe Ted doesn't even suspect Sebastian and they are just going to Europe because the police might find out Ted was the threatener.'

The more they talked about it, the more clear it seemed that Sebastian must have done the deed, intentionally or by chance, for love of Ted. They told each other everything they might have neglected to share, starting with Gen's return to the States and ending with her account of the imaginary death scene. Carl set her straight on Romeo and Juliet. It was Juliet, not Romeo, who lay in a 'seeming death', and when Romeo saw her so he quaffed off some quick-acting poison.

Carl demonstrated by emptying his glass of champagne, kissing Gen's hand, and tumbling off the sofa, saying, 'Thus with a kiss I die.' He closed his eyes and was still.

Even knowing he was fooling, Gen felt a wave of grief. I will not survive this man's death, she thought.

Carl rolled on to his side and propped himself up on one elbow. Gen looked away, suddenly shy to let him see in her eyes how much she loved him. 'So you see,' he said, 'there was no blood. Therefore, if I had woken and seen you with a knife in your bosom, I wouldn't have known what you meant by it. Especially since I'd only been napping. I'd never put the two together. Gen kills herself because Carl has a snooze? It doesn't make sense!' He jumped to his feet, grabbed a newspaper, and read aloud, '*Famous Musician Found Asleep. Lover Kills Self.*'

When they'd finished laughing, they took a solemn oath never to have secrets from each other but always to be open and truthful and utterly trusting.

They heard Rick and Laura's voices from the hall. Gen said hastily, almost desperately, 'But, sweetheart, about this Sebastian business. It's all just guesswork on our part. Since Ted and he will probably stay together regardless, and it is Laura's home, don't you think it's better. . .'

'Not to tell Laura?' he inquired ominously.

'Yes,' she said gratefully.

'No, I do not think it is better.' He scowled at her. 'No.' He frowned ferociously. 'You promised you'd tell her things from now on.'

'I know, but . . .'

'This is a real problem with you. We have just been saying how important is it not to keep things from one's intimates. We vowed. We took an oath!'

'I know. . .'

Laura entered the room. 'Oh, Mom, you look so much better.' She came and gave her kiss, and sat with her arm around her shoulder.

'Your mother has something to tell you,' Carl said.

Laura looked expectant. Gen looked agonized. 'I think

205

– Carl and I both think – that Sebastian might have been the one who beat up Jim.'

'I'm afraid I think so, too,' Laura said, obviously relieved to be able to talk about it. 'He knows how much Ted loves me, and something he said led me to believe he knew about Jim. Poor Sebastian. He's very emotional. He has no control. Maybe Dad will encourage him to stay in Europe. I hope so. I'm so relieved you thought the same thing and I'm not alone in my suspicions.'

Carl looked smugly at Gen as if to say, 'See, you did the right thing.' Then he told Laura how they'd come to their conclusion, and Laura filled in with more thoughts that had been plaguing her. The three of them talked together like a family.

'Now tell Laura the other thing,' Carl said happily.

Gen looked terribly apprehensive, much more so than before. 'Oh dear,' she said tremulously. 'Which other thing?'

She appeared to have a mental block about their betrothal. Carl helped her out. 'The thing about our engagement,' he said patiently.

She lit up. 'We're engaged to be married,' she said. 'I hope you'll be happy for us.'

'I am, Mom. I'm very glad. I know I've been difficult about Carl and I'm sorry. I'm beginning to see that he really is good for you – and for me, too,' she added generously.

'Will you play Laura the song?'

Carl played the song again. He thought, this is it. I'm completely happy. Life begins. I have my music, my Genevieve, and Laura's blessing at last. I really must owe God a lot for this. I wonder if He'll take a cheque.

When the applause died down, Gen said, 'Now shall I tell Laura the other thing?'

It was Carl's turn to look puzzled. 'What other thing?'

'Laura, honey, let me just whisper something to Carl.' Laura left the sofa as Carl approached. When she was out of earshot, Gen whispered into Carl's ear, 'Shall I tell

Laura you sank my houseboat?'

'Are you kidding? No. Absolutely not.'

'No?' Gen affected surprise. 'What about openness and truthfulness among loved ones? What about vows and oaths and promises?'

'Laura likes me now. It would not be a good thing for her to know. She would never understand. Anyhow, it doesn't really concern her.'

'I think it does concern her,' Gen whispered. 'And I did promise her. And didn't you once say that a buried truth becomes foul and slimy . . .?'

'Listen!' Carl grabbed her arms so hard she gasped. 'If you ever, *ever* tell Laura I sank your houseboat, I'll kill you.'

Gen was silent, impressed. Carl was impressed, too. He still hadn't once used the Nautalis machine.

She rubbed her arms. 'OK,' she conceded. She paused, then whispered, 'But shall I tell Laura the other thing?'

'Good grief!' Carl said aloud in exasperation. He hit his head with his hand, stood up, spread his arms, gave up trying to maintain a whisper and cried, 'I can't believe this! What other thing? There is no other thing!' He began to flail his arms and dry his hands.

'Come on, you guys,' Laura said, sick of waiting discreetly at the far end of the room. 'Tell me.'

'Well,' Gen began, grabbing one of Carl's hands as it winged her way. 'This is something really amazing and wonderful that concerns you both. We're going to have a baby.'

It was Carl's turn to faint. He swooned dead away.

When he came to in Gen's arms, he thought exuberantly, this woman will always surprise me. A baby! Of both of ours! We combined to make a little human being. A greenhorn!

But when he spoke, he said, 'I will never know if the baby's not really Rick's. Never.'

Gen laughed and tried to grab his arms hard. 'If you ever, *ever* tell our baby I slept with Rick . . .'

'Our baby,' Carl said. 'Imagine!'

He got a singular look on his face that Gen had sometimes particularly noticed and wondered about. She ven-
tured a guess. 'While you're at it, thank Him for me.'

Carl gave her a look of unutterable happiness because
she apparently knew the one thing he hadn't been able,
and didn't seem to know how, to tell her.